Gentling Soul

A LEGACY OF LOVE

El Alma

BALBOA.PRESS
A DIVISION OF HAY HOUSE

Balboa Press books may be ordered through booksellers or by contacting:

Balboa Press
A Division of Hay House
1663 Liberty Drive
Bloomington, IN 47403
www.balboapress.com.au
AU TFN: 1 800 844 925 (Toll Free inside Australia)
AU Local: (02) 8310 7086 (+61 2 8310 7086 from outside Australia)

Print information available on the last page.

ISBN: 978-1-9822-9834-0 (sc)
ISBN: 978-1-9822-9835-7 (e)

Balboa Press rev. date: 10/09/2023

only love unites us

Contents

Introduction

Have you ever met someone who unnerves your equilibrium? This is a truly genuine and humble person who fully lives in his or her soul, a soul who has chosen to spend an earth's lifetime wholly being a soul within an impaired body.

Have you turned away from such a person, unable to process the emotional disturbance in you? Or have you grappled with your emotions and tried to understand and tried to communicate?

You know this person is not dangerous to you physically and is not verbally abusive to you. In fact, the person will not likely harm you in any way, other than for the unpleasant social moment he or she tries to interact with you.

When you meet the person, you sense the person is from another realm than you. You try quickly to focus your attention on understanding the person's language even though he or she speaks the same local dialect as you.

This person is very awkward socially and will possibly turn his or her eyes away from you, even though he or she wants so much to communicate. The grunts or mumbled and sometimes incoherent words are the best the person can produce in this anxious situation. The person tries so hard to form sentences in your language.

All in all, this person is usually inept at striking up a fluent conversation with you. While you find a mutual level, where you can both understand each other, the conversation tapers off and finally ends. You know you did the best you could, and you walk away relieved that the interaction is over. You dismiss the conversation from your mind.

The awkward and humble person walks away. The person tried the best he or she could, and the person knows intuitively he or she has been misunderstood again. The person leaves you and waits for the next interaction that could happen within moments.

This social awkwardness will repeat when the person needs to interact with someone else walking down the street, or in a shopping centre, or in any gathering of people.

Therefore, these people tend to wait in the shadows in social settings, where they have been designated to by those who can't cope with them. Or they stay at home choosing not to do the "meet and greet thing" as it takes great courage and willpower for these people to want to socialize.

Who are these people I'm talking to you about?

They are the ones with neurogenetic disorders, inherited physiological disorders coupled with neurological impairment.

They belong in every other family you may know. They are the ones who have been left out of the mainstream of society until recent years. You see them coming to the forefront now in sports, school settings, and social settings. However, it still takes the public's breath away when they are seen in relationships, or participating in sporting events, or establishing careers.

They overwhelm us with anxiety for them. We look from a distance and wonder about their existence and thank God that is not us or one of our children or our family.

We are so fortunate that we don't have to handle that, we say to ourselves.

Yet their parents and families adjust as best they can throughout the years to their language, their emotions, their physical weaknesses, their overt and covert behaviours, and their unnerving presence. Some families find it impossible to adjust.

Are you squirming now, saying to yourself, *I don't want to read about this stuff. It's not relevant to me.* Even if it is relevant, you may be saying, "I can't cope with talking about this topic anymore. It will always be the same."

This story is not about the proverbial uncomfortable and unsolvable situations you find yourself in or you find others in. This story is a generational tale that begins long ago and far away in the motherland of the characters where truth lies dormant for generations. It takes one gentling soul to go to the past in search of the beginnings of the seed of misfortune. Or is it a seed of hope planted all those years ago and is only now opening to the full light of the truth?

Then you may ask, "Who is a 'gentling soul'?"

A "gentling soul" is defined in the story as one who has chosen to come to earth to speak an urgent message in the language of the soul, a language foreign to the masses on earth.

A "gentling soul" can be compared to a "horse gentler," one who works with horses and will gently tame them, not using the whip to break them in. A "gentling soul" comes to gently tame and quiet souls and brings them to their own souls' purposes.

A "gentling soul" is one who is unlike others. He or she has chosen not to fit into society, but to stand outside society and yet live in society. They speak loudest through their need to be loved, accepted, and understood, to be cared for by us, and to be seen as their souls' purposes.

They are here to take us on a journey away from the expectations of a "normal" life; to show us simplicity, genuineness, kindness, awkwardness, softness, gentleness, empathy, compassion, and love.

Frequently asked questions about them include, "Why are they on earth? Where do they fit in to our society?"

The scientific answer is they have genetic anomalies that occur in human, animal, and plant life. The common medical solution is that these anomalies need to be alleviated through cures and/or chosen to be bred out.

But is there a spiritual answer? Or is there a spiritual question?

As most "gentling souls" are almost unable to even exist on the earth with their excessive sensitivities to their physical senses, could it be spiritually implied then that they are meant to be here in these times? These are times of war, terrorism, global disease, the uncovering of abuse by those in authority, consumerism, and drug and alcohol abuse.

This is a tale of a family of gentling souls. One gentling soul, Asina, speaks out and tries to attain understanding for the gentling souls. There is disbelief as this sincere soul steps from within the ranks of the status quo. People ask, "How can he or she be a mentor?"

Her story begins at a gathering of souls taking place in heaven many earth years prior to this present life. The soul of Asina is part of the assembly where she and her family members are choosing to come to earth with impairments and are agreeing to their specific times to enter the earth's atmosphere.

The souls of her family members who do not choose the impairment instead choose to enter and be part of the influx of the gentling souls as their companions, to understand, love, protect, and support the impaired ones while on earth.

The story follows the gentling souls' journeys to earth and concludes in the present time. The gentling souls who have come to earth in such large numbers in Asina's family come to understand through their intertwined stories why they are here.

Asina describes how a genetic disorder is inherited and the impact on the family who are found to have a genetic disorder in their lineage. She also describes how the family come to live with the impairment, and how they find hope and love and peace living as gentling souls and as companion souls.

As this is not a medical research paper, it does not name the genetic anomaly found in the story. You may wish to search relevant research papers for further information regarding genetic disorders.

Chapter 1

ACCEPTANCE

Drifting in and out of sleep while seated in my favourite armchair in the late evening, I am being drawn into my peaceful space between asleep and awake. Ever so gently, I begin to feel my soul journeying in the company of my heavenly travel companion to an ancient era before this present life on earth.

Silently she tells me, "I am leading you to a heavenly event of long ago where you are attending a conclave of many souls. Open your soul's memory, Asina. Remember who you are. Remember choosing your soul's intention that you accepted long before this present existence."

I am now moving in a profoundly deep and mystical energy with her, but curiously I have no recollection of this conclave she urgently wishes me to remember. Radiating beams of light upon and through me, she enters a magnificent chamber filled with multi-coloured beams of light. She guides me to a huge meeting where many stunning light beings are assembled in deep discussion.

The engaging entities bow to the instant presence of their heavenly Mother. She gestures them to encourage me to take part in their deliberation. As instructed by the entities, I am being ushered to descend into their midst to accept my place of long ago. Slowly I merge down into their presence and realise I am no longer an earthly body, but a being of light immersed in their spirit and in the love of their heavenly Mother once more.

My memory arouses thoughts of a past commitment with this gathering of souls, a commitment I am told that I made with them nearly two earth centuries ago. As I plunge my soul deep into the fullness of the group, the intense purpose of the light beings holding such a summit opens in me. Increasingly I recognise I am with my own soul family as a crucial arrangement is being formed in heaven with souls who are choosing to be the future arrivals in our family of souls on earth.

Silently, the Divine Spirit speaks to me of the great proposal intended for my family of souls. "Your family of souls is preparing for the next global transformations."

Ahh! Yes, I remember. *The discussion is for my soul family to accept the intention of the enhancement of our own souls, as well as for the enhancement for other souls who will be entering the earth's future.*

Instantly, the ancient ceremony expands into a silent vision of the future earth opening in front of us. Many of the souls who are present in the image are within the assembly of the many light beings.

The image unveils great wars, starvation, poverty, and diseases running rampant throughout the peoples of many countries on earth, particularly in the lands of my earthly ancestors. We are shown my peoples' lack of food and I hear the prediction of how malnourishment and addictive substances will change their bodily functions in the future. I envision their souls becoming more and more supressed and their bodies more and more depressed.

We are also shown the many continuing earth battles culminating in the desolation of humanity. We foresee the displacement of survivors, and the refugees from many lands trying to find new lands to inhabit.

We see the destruction of the earth's environment, and the fearsome change it creates in the climate for her cities and country regions. Opening before us we see great sicknesses creeping throughout all the countries of the earth, infecting and killing millions of people.

Within their submission, the council of light beings proposes to our family of souls, "You will prepare to enter earth for these determining times by choosing a significant and specific impairment to the body that will develop because of generations of change to your earthly bodies.

"The impairment will allow you to remain as your 'souls' while on earth in the hope of lovingly enthusing other humans gently to their own souls. Each of you as an impaired soul, a gentling soul, will make sure the generations of gentling souls, the lowly ones, will continue to bring peace to the future. You will create and continue to initiate the arrival of many gentling souls, who will increase during almost two centuries of new arrivals continuing to the present day."

I understand immediately that I am already an integral part of the elders' strategy. I absorb the words of the council: "Your family members who choose to come to earth with impairments, thus creating gentle souls, will agree to enter the earth's environment during a specific upcoming historical event."

An elder of the council continues, "Your family members who do not choose the impairment for themselves will choose instead to come as companions and to be part of the influx of gentling souls. They will understand, love, protect, and support each gentling soul while on earth."

The conference culminates in a unanimous acceptance by my family of souls to the proposal presented by the presiding elders. Together with my family, I agree to collaborate with the wise ones and with one another. We reply in unison, "We will come as gentle souls through a genetic impairment. The gentle ones will arrive in accordance with the heavenly plan to infuse the earth with innocent

3

goodness, knowing that we as the gentling souls will either be accepted, annihilated, or bred out."

The elder continues, "The agreement forged between heaven and earth by the gentling souls and the presiding light beings will occur during great depressions on the earth's inhabitants caused by famine, wars, diseases, displacement, abuse, and materialism. The gentling souls and their protectors will come to filter goodness and blessings onto the earth throughout the repressed coming generations."

Having been made fully aware of the ongoing schedule and how the existing course of events is presently emerging, I belong again with the ancient light beings who originally assisted my family of many gentling souls to formulate and execute the heavenly plan.

I am shown that the plan has now spread through many other families of gentling souls to every corner of the earthly globe. In all countries, the gentling souls try to survive earth's cruelty to the sensitivities of their bodies, minds, and souls.

Upon our souls' acceptance of the agreement between heaven and earth, I instantly feel a tremendous shift in energy as a movement of souls takes flight and rises from the earth. Like a huge flock of birds flying in tight formation, the lead souls soar higher. Together we twist and turn through pockets of downdraughts, avoiding vortices that could annihilate our very beings.

Suddenly our flock rapidly changes course and turns downwards in tight formation. All souls sense the massive energy hurtling us towards annihilation. If one of us drops out of formation, we will be left to struggle back into the fast-flowing stream of air alone.

Intuitively, we know to wait for an upward pressure to be able to ascend once more. The energy shifts to avoid mass destruction and deep within the energy of global consciousness, I soar upwards once more with the souls of love.

With all my strength, I hold tight and become one with the gentling souls and our soul family. I believe this shift will avert a global pandemic, political upheavals, continuing wars, and annihilation of the masses with nuclear weapons. I know that not a single hair of our heads will go unnoticed as I fervently seek Spirit. *"Are we not more than the birds of the sky?"*

Slowly, I rouse from my half-sleep state, and struggle to process the experience I have just come through. Immediately, I grab my beads and start murmuring the rosary. It seems days since I have picked them up to pray. I finish two full cycles of the beads and begin to process my visit to the conclave of souls and the enormity of the shift of the global consciousness.

As I become fully aware of my earthly body again, I believe this great revelation from heaven, predominantly functioning within the great heavenly movement of gentling souls on earth, is possible. We are gentling souls who have come to gentle many souls to bring calmness, peace, and love to the planet during many different lifetimes.

Regaining my earthly perspective, I also remember we have been in isolation, locked away from the uncontrolled global contagion. Sentel and I had shut our business weeks earlier, leaving us with no income. We are both feeling desperate and extremely agitated when contemplating our sudden move out of our business of twenty-five years due to our health and age.

However, after the many long lockdowns, we are again opening and working our business with staff in-store, while the two of us are working from the safety of our home.

My poor mind is grappling to comprehend the unprecedented events happening in the world and the synchronisation with the conclave of souls. I seek clarity on how to make any needed strategic moves as I ponder all circumstances.

Spirit remains silently translating to me the synchronisation of the events of the conclave and the earthly demise of many of its inhabitants moving together. Spirit reveals, "An earthly fear has become the mainstay of global societies and is now presenting itself in every aspect of daily life. This massive collective energy of fear is regurgitating itself over and over until it is spilling into family and social life and through political and financial dealings in global systems.

"The fear can be seen within the minds of the earth's inhabitants. It is becoming uncontrollable and changing the earth through the pollution in the air, the oceans, and waterways across all lands. The media is portraying the fear in terms of mass anger, revenge, bitterness, and hatred that is rife in the world. The fear has become the catalyst for all the other emotions.

"The fear has become so fixed in the collective mind. Humans have created an energy so profound that it has formed into an uncontrollable global consciousness of fear in human thoughts and actions. This tremendous fear has become a tangible entity in the form of terrorism and the threat of global nuclear war."

Sadly, I see what Spirit is saying. We are being attacked by the fear through our relationships, the very core of who we are. The onslaught of our fear is the poison that is creating destruction beyond anything we have witnessed. It incorporates every citizen of the earth. No one is exempt. We need to see our mistakes but not dally there in the past too long. We need to look forward and to focus on our way out of the fear.

Instantly, I hear Spirit say, "Replace fear with love. It is the time for you all to reflect on yourselves as more than human beings. You are eternal beings. Your consciousnesses exist eternally. Your souls are the love of God. Love with your whole soul, your whole heart, and your whole mind. Love each other."

Spirit instructs me, "The collective global consciousness has been summoned during this time to peacefully overcome the threat of global fear and disorder. All measures are being placed on earth by humble souls so that cooperation and self-sacrifices will endure for the good of all.

"No one is exempt from duty, especially not the spiritual light workers both on earth and in heaven. They are flying in a massive formation of intention and fervour to meet the chaos head on with a force to annihilate the fear. Activate spiritual front line workers. They must summon all souls together with the intention of overcoming this attack on humanity.

"For it is through the quiet gentling souls that there comes the acceptance of His love for us. He uses the gentling souls as His faithful servants who have not availed themselves of the many unattainable desires and need for control presented in this life for others. They are left unscarred by the search for lives that will take them far from their souls. They are left only with their souls within impaired bodies."

Chapter 2

PAST LIVES

Weeks and months pass, and I am back to my daily chores with the memory of the conclave of souls ever present in my mind. We are both still in isolation during the pandemic due to health and age issues, and I spend each day with questions without answers. The confusion begins to disrupt my in-between sleep and awake periods. Again I travel to a time long ago and a place I recognise from my visit to the conclave. I recognise I am existing in the old world of my homeland with, I come to believe, my ancestors—souls I have encountered at the conclave.

In this present time travel event, these souls become my immediate family, and I am waking with them early on a cold winter's morning over a century ago. I am experiencing a past life as Hana, a little girl about ten years old.

I am stirring in my bed just before the light breaks open the sky for the sun to shine upon the earth. I jump up quickly, rug up in my warm clothes, and rush outside to watch the golden light rise over the green mountains.

I wait anxiously for the light to touch the valley below as I think on today. *This is the last time I will see the sunrise in my home country. I will put a picture of it in my mind and place this picture deep into my memory to hold this last moment of my home in my soul forever. I know I will never return to this home, and I need to remember this picture for the many years to come in our new country.*

As Asina, I have become enthralled in my unfolding regression to a past life as the little girl. I am Hana, standing at her front gate on the side of the hill overlooking the dead pastures that have not been able to feed the family. I watch as the fast-flowing water gushes through the fields and pours over the dead crops. I become fascinated by the rain from the night before as it rushes down the hills to join the flood of water spilling into the river.

Gazing into the future, remembering the past, and holding the present moment in my mind, I sadly say to myself, *This farming area has been home to my parents, and to grandparents from both sides and their parents and grandparents before them. Now it is time for us to prepare to leave the country where we were born and set sail for a faraway land.*

But the excitement of starting fresh in a new land is becoming filled with sad feelings of saying goodbye to my family, including Pa's parents, who I will never see again. My beloved Granny and Papa are being left behind, and only Ma's parents and her sister will come with us.

All my child worries and my child wonders fill my head as I hear the birds waking up and I see the sun peeking through the cloudy sky. "Whatever will become of us?" I cry to Jesus.

"Hana, come and eat. We need to finish packing our boxes of belongings and load them onto the carts."

Ma breaks my thoughts and feelings and wakes the others.

"Coming Ma," I call back, running to the house.

I help Ma make the last scraps of dry bread into a measly breakfast. She soaks the bread in the warm, fresh milk she has just taken from the only cow that we are leaving for the others in the family. She sprinkles a little sugar on the bread to sweeten the food.

Ma settles the family at the table and reminds us, "Now you know Pa is already in Australia for nearly three years. During that time, he has found paid work on a farm that has adequate accommodation for all of us, and he has already paid for our journey across the sea. We have all missed him since he sailed on his own to etch out our future. It will be so good for us all to be together again.

"You know Nanny and Pop and Mara are also coming with us on our journey to support me with all you children and to also settle with us in Australia. I want you to be very good for them and do as they tell you as we travel our long journey together."

"Yes Ma, we know all that and yes, we will be good. All I can think about is arriving in Australia to see Pa again," I blurt out boldly.

With great excitement, we all gather the treasures we want to take with us and pack them in the one big wooden box made empty just for our precious belongings. Amongst Nanny's few treasures, a precious painting of her helper Saint Anthony is balancing against the box, waiting to be packed. Nanny told me that she was given the painting by her mother before she passed. She told me that she will pass it to Ma to protect her and help her family in their new life when she passes. Ma promised she will pass it to me one day before she goes home to Jesus.

We leave the table, clean up the kitchen, and pack any scraps of bread left over and any other utensils we will need. We hurry to gather our belongings. We make many trips to the horse-drawn carts and carriages that belong to relatives and neighbours who are arriving to help to get us to the wharves before midday. Ma has told us that our ship sails on the high tide in the early evening.

When we are all done, we make our last passage through the gates of our home. The long line of grandparents, aunts, uncles, and neighbours follow us to the wharf to say goodbye and to wish us happiness in our new country.

Pa's mother hugs me and tells me, "Give your father a hug for me. I won't see him again. Look after him. It is up to you children to work and survive in a foreign land. We are too old to come with you." She also warns us, "It will take a long time to get our farming land well again." I walk away from her understanding that the family we are leaving behind have decided to leave the farm and move to the cities to find work instead of coming with us to a new land.

Hana's new life is only beginning as I wake from my journey to the homeland. Upon waking, my half-opened eyes fall on the painting of Saint Anthony residing for years above my bedhead. The painting was given to me many years ago by my paternal ancestors through Hana.

I now know that it is my three times great grandmother's painting passed down within the family along my paternal grandmother's side. I whisper to myself in wonder, "All those women have had that painting above their bedheads throughout their lifetimes, as I do now."

The realisation of the ancient painting still in my possession urges me to again ponder the purse that my maternal grandmother Ezara left to me. Ezara's purse was used as a receptacle for the little money Ezara had when I was a child growing up with her. In this moment, I realise that both my maternal grandmother and my paternal grandmother are of great significance in my present life. During the next few weeks, in my quiet times, I reminisce on the years since the passing of Ezara. I feel joy in my soul when I think of her, and realise to this day I still keep my rose-perfumed rosary beads in her little black purse.

My thoughts remind me that my beads and the little purse have now become worn from long use. Both have become very fragile, and each time I use the beads, I become fearful that the purse and the chain on the beads might break completely.

My thoughts push me to urgent action. *I should find another container for the beads as I may lose some of the beads that fall off occasionally.*

With that thought I set about tidying my bedroom drawers and cabinet to find a suitable container for the beads.

Going through my possessions thoughtfully one by one, I come across a little silk purse that once contained a black pearl pendant. Silently, I draw my daughter into my heart. *Nettie, you gave this pendant to me just before you were diagnosed with terminal cancer.*

Sadness fills me awhile until I realise, *I always wear the pendant from this unused purse, so it is an ideal receptacle even though it is not a little "black" purse.* I hold the purse in my hands and look at a reddish-purple coloured purse and think, *What a shame it is not black. Still, I will use it regardless of the colour.* Instantly, I feel the connection between Nettie and Ezara become one with me in my soul again.

With all these thoughts in my mind, the day slowly progresses into night. I prepare the evening meal for the family of six. After it is eaten and cleaned up, I finally shower and dress for sleep. I read in bed for a while, but I remain unsettled, and I soon realise that I will not be going to sleep just yet.

I throw my feet out of the bed and grab my warm gown and slippers. I make my way back out to the kitchen again. Everyone else has gone to bed, so I make a cup of hot tea and sit down in my comfy chair. I am guided by Spirit to listen clearly to what it is that is calling me to attention.

I sit and contemplate on my wandering thoughts in the semi-dark until I feel ready to articulate my needs to Spirit. "Please guide me to your divine plan. Please let me know somehow that it is your will that I immerse my soul in the quest of the great conclave of souls. Is the purpose of the gentling souls' presence here on earth to enlighten others? Are both the little black purse and Saint Anthony's painting crucially imbued faith touchstones to my gentling soul's mission?

"I need a sign that will help me to know that these are your directives. Are all these messages real or are they 'my imaginings'? I fervently need an answer from you, Divine Spirit, Jesus, and Mother Mary. Thank you."

I don't fully know exactly what I need. It is all just thoughts floating around in my mind. Suddenly, one flashing thought passes through me, *a shooting star!*

Now I hear in my thoughts, *Midnight!*

How could I order one of them at midnight? I laugh to myself.

I get up and walk off thinking to myself, *It is just a thought.*

On my way out of the kitchen walking towards the door, I look at the time. It is 11.35 p.m. I think, *Mm, I can get a rosary in before midnight.*

I turn off the lights and walk to my bedroom along the long veranda in the light of the full moon to get my rosary beads, my perfumed ones in the little reddish-purple purse. I don't turn on any lights as I reach under my pillow, pick up the silk purse, and open it in the dark. I feel inside with my fingers, take out the beads, and smell them and the purse. They are so richly perfumed, really *perfumed!*

Now I know Mary is close, as she always perfumes my beads when she seeks me out.

I come back to the veranda, and I notice the bathroom light is still on. I leave it on to see as I walk down the small staircase to the outside chair on the grass. I sit in the chair in the country courtyard that is facing the same area where I have placed Mary's statue. The bathroom light and the moon shine gently on my surrounds as I begin the rosary slowly.

Soon someone turns the light off inside the house, not realising I am out in the courtyard. I am left only the light of the moon. I do not move a muscle. Thoughts of a snake sliding over my feet and legs penetrate my fears. I decide if that happens, I will just sit still and cringe.

At the last bead of the last decade, I turn my gaze to the right above the huge tree in the farmyard. An amazingly large shooting star suddenly appears right in front of me. It flashes so close to me that I hear the crack of its entrance passing through from the celestial sphere. It is a magnificent white light with a shooting tail that disappears behind the tree. The moment is Divine and overwhelming.

In that split second, Jesus and Mary tell me everything I need to know. They are ever present. I check the time and it is exactly midnight.

I sit still, frozen in the sanctified moment for a long while watching the darkened sky. I am completely astonished and ever so grateful. I feel intensely protected and loved by God.

Slowly, I rise from the chair and walk back to my bedroom along the long veranda in the moonlight. I smell my beads and realise the strong perfume of the beads is beginning to fade. I open the bedroom door leading from the veranda and I find my torch in the usual place near my pillow. I turn it on to find the purse under the pillow to put my beads back.

I shine the torch under my pillow, and I take out the purse. Now I am truly astounded. The purse is now fully black in the light of the torch. It is not the reddish-purple colour it was when I last saw the purse in the light. I look at the purse in extreme shock.

I gasp out loud to no one there, only Jesus and Mary, "It is now black—it is so black! It has the same gold markings still on it."

I have been given my own little black purse with all Mother Mary's teachings and blessings in it. I silently squeal with utter shock and excitement, not wanting to wake anyone. I climb back into bed and curl up in the foetal position, shaking with excitement, gratitude, and awe that will last with me forever.

O so gently, I fall into a deep state knowing my earthly mother's teachings and love remain concealed in the little black purse together with Mother Mary's blessings and the teachings of her Son's love for humanity.

Both Jesus and Mary endorse the crucial importance of the existence of the conclave of souls of centuries ago. They acknowledge the existence of the little black purse. And they are preparing the way for me to understand the existence of the painting of Saint Anthony and the existence of the gentling souls. I also feel encouraged with fleeting thoughts of wonderment of who the next keepers of the little black purse and the painting are going to be.

Chapter 3

SETTING SAIL

Weeks after the shooting star experience, much exploration into my family's history is beginning. Once more, I travel with my heavenly companions back to visit as Hana and become immersed in the family's life. On my arrival, I find we are at the wharf, where the family and I are preparing to depart on the ship to Australia.

All passengers are eager to get their luggage and themselves onto the ship through the formal process of leaving the homeland. We children are gathered around the adults, who are herding all of us into in a tight group where we are unable to wander and get lost. Mari gives us water and bread to keep us fed and occupied as all the adults cope with handling the luggage.

We stay together as we are told to do. We stand and watch as each of our boxes is loaded onto pallets then hoisted with huge ropes high onto the ship's decks. We all feel the rush of people around us. We hear the noise of the ship's workers, the yelling of passengers to each other, and the constant hollering of directions on board and on land. All this happens alongside the thunderous roar of the ship's engines turning over. Leaving our homeland becomes an unforgettable moment.

After watching the men load the ship with our belongings, it is now that we have to say goodbye. I am feeling anxious and sick with mixed feelings: sadness at saying goodbye to my family who are staying behind and the excitement of finally boarding the ship bound to cross the seas to be with my father again.

We are boarding at last, and all the passengers' farewells are happening as they take their places along the railings up and down the full length of the ship. My salty tears pour down my cheeks as the sea salt begins to stick to my face and hair.

I travel to the present for a moment as Asina, look at the happenings of long ago, and muse. *By the time we reach our destination, we will all feel the full impact of living on the sea: the endless nausea; the unsteady movement that will disturb our bodies' balance; the crammed living conditions with strangers who will either become lifetime friends or enemies, or remain strangers; the changing weather conditions from calm seas to terrifying vortices of raging water whipped by torrential rain and gale force winds; the restlessness and illnesses of adults and children; and the endless days and nights of suspenseful drama accompanied by broken sleep.*

Instantly, I'm whisked back to settling into our designated cabins. They can barely hold two adults let alone three of us in each, even if most of us are only little. The children are grouped into pairs and the adults are separated, giving each pair our own caregiver who will be responsible for us. The cramped areas quickly become strewn with articles of clothing, blankets, and personal belongings.

At last, the ship sets sail and makes its way out through the harbour into the open sea on dusk and the full tide. As the pace picks up, we all feel a sense of relief. We all finish the left-over bread and biscuits and wash the food down with water. After setting up our own beds, we climb under the covers to sleep.

In the morning, there are stomach aches, sea sickness from the constant movement of the water, growing boredom, and irritableness from lack of sleep amongst us all. Ma tells us, "Get out onto the decks. It is more pleasurable than being locked up in the cabins. We will only choose to spend the darkness of the nights behind closed doors. Food is up on deck, but it is scarce and is to be shared between all. Please stay with your adult."

Days follow days and nights become more stifling in the cabins. We have a routine and it is working for us, and no one has been lost yet. We forget how long it really has been that we have been on the ship. Time seems to drag slowly with no change in weather or the routine.

Then one afternoon just before dark, we are warned by the captain over the loudspeaker that there is bad weather ahead. We are told we need to go to the cabins and remain off the decks. Instantly there is panic among the adults, and they gather us, as I have seen them herd the sheep at home, into the stifling cabins.

It is raining as darkness comes on us. We hear the thunder and see the flashes of lightning through the portholes. The seas are surging and lifting the ship out of the water. The ship arches high above the waves. The angry sea smashes against the side of the ship as it drops off the next wave and the next wave. Everything is moving in our room and our belongings are flying weapons. We are all screaming now. The adults try their best to hold onto us and to calm us as the sea pounds us like Ma pounds the dough for bread.

Then one of us retches and another follows. The stench is revolting and Nanny cries out to us, "We need to ride out the storm before anyone can be attended to."

It seems like hours before the thrashing of the water against the ship begins to ease. No one is left standing. We are exhausted and most of us are left with empty stomachs. I am crying, along with all the children. Ma begins, "I know we are all in a mess. Stop crying now children. We are all safe and we can clean up and start again. Come now, let's get out of your smelly clothes. We'll get to the showers, wash, put on clean clothes, and then we'll feel better."

Ma takes us to the bathrooms while Mara and Nanny and Pop try to clean the cabins. "We might even get some sleep when we get back to the cabins. You know that this is the first of many storms we will meet before we reach land. We will know what to do next time," Ma tells us on the way back to our cabins.

"Next time?" I question, as all the children jump in to echo my moaning. "We are all wanting the journey to be over, Ma!"

But Ma tells me, "Even when the journey ends, it will take us time to recover from the effects on our bodies from the sea. We will feel like we are still on the sea for days after. We will also need to undergo the long immigration procedures before we are even free to set out to travel the strange country's soil."

Most of the clean-up of the cabin is done when we get back from our baths still complaining. It takes most of the next day to air out our belongings and get things back the way they were. Ma was right: as another storm a few days later upends our normality again. We all notice that with each storm, the weather is getting hotter and hotter as we travel into the warmer climate closer to Australia.

It is becoming even too hot to sleep in the cabins, and we all try to sleep on the deck chairs outside in the cool breeze. The main clothes we have with us are useless in the heat, so Ma cuts off sleeves of dresses and shirts, and legs off trousers so our bodies can feel the cool air.

Days pass slowly. By now, we have had enough of the sea and the ship and the hot sun. Then rising early one morning Ma calls to us. "Look, there is land ahead! It is Australia," she says. Each of us races to the deck, hangs off the railings, and stands, watching as the land gets closer and closer.

The sky is blue, and the sun is hot as we slowly approach the coastline. Ma reports, "It is nothing like home. The sand is yellow, and the waters are so blue. It is a hot summer day in the new country as we finally reach the shores of our new home."

Excitement fills the air. It seems all the passengers are glad the journey is over as they run backwards and forwards and from side to side of the ship, trying to get a glimpse of the new land. We are all weather-beaten, burnt by the sun, and exhausted as we, with all the passengers, walk off the ship onto solid ground.

"Now," Ma says, "we need to go through the major challenge of the immigration process, which is going to take what will feel like forever to us."

We are put in a run-down section of the port and during the long hours' wait, we have plenty of time to begin to try to feel our land legs again. Ma tells us, "It will take even more time before everything eventually stops swaying in our bodies, but the experience of the sea will be with us for a lifetime."

At last, we are lined up to catch a train to travel west for hours nearer to the farm Pa has found for us as our new home. As our train pulls into the station, we, as bedraggled sailors, soon have our belongings loaded onto the train. We board and find our seats. We are finally out of the sun and settling on the train for the night.

The heat is awful, but we already know to wear almost nothing as we did on the ship when we felt the heat of the warm waters. The train journey is long for all of us, but at least it is cooler with the windows down as we travel through the night.

Travelling farther and farther inland, our trip has become the first experience in this huge, hot, and dusty land that is nothing like the cool and green land we have left behind. We realise that the clothes we have with us are useless for this extremely hot, dry land. Ma tells us, "We will need cool cotton clothes, boots to walk in and to work the land, and broad-brimmed hats. The first job when we get settled will be buying and making suitable clothes for the heat and to learn how to acclimatise to the weather."

As we pull into the country station the next morning, we see Pa, who has travelled from the farm, sitting alone waiting for us. As we get off the train one by one, we each rush to hug him. We are all so excited to see him as we mull together on the platform. Before long, our tears are flowing, with raucous laughter and silly giggling releasing our relief and exhaustion.

But our gathering is over quickly as Pa rushes off to help with our luggage and get it loaded onto the back of the huge cart he has brought to take us to our new home. We all scramble to get onto the cart at once with Pa, to travel the last part of the journey. The journey to our new home continues.

Pa leads the horses out onto the wide-open road. Leaving the morning sun behind us, he heads in the opposite direction towards where the sun will set. It seems the flat land runs forever in every direction as the few town houses disappear. The land is not green and lush like in our valley of home. This land is dry and brown and dusty. The heat makes the dust stick to our sweaty bodies and leaves streams of muddy brown water flowing down our faces, arms, and legs.

I look at Pa holding the reins and I see his skin has changed colour. He is not white like us anymore. His skin is as brown as the dirt, his face is wrinkled with grooves made by the streams of brown sweat, and his hands are hard and burnt from the sun. I look at the mountains in the distance and they have a blue tinge to them. There seems to be a long range of mountains on the horizon laid out before us that stretches as far as I can see to the left and to the right of me.

"How far is it to the farmhouse, Pa?" I ask.

"A day's ride from here, Hana. We will be there just before dark."

With that information, I settle on top of one of our boxes on the cart and get as comfortable as possible. I watch everything that moves. I stare off into the distance and watch the mountains to see if they get any closer.

Chapter 4

AUSTRALIA

We arrive at the farmhouse late in the afternoon dusty, exhausted, and excited at the same time. We drag our belongings off the farm cart and scatter in every direction. I walk with Ma up the steps into her new home with Pa. She smiles with tears in her eyes as she sees he has already set up the house for us.

I watch as Ma turns to Pa, takes his hand, places her head on his shoulder, and cries quietly into his dusty shirt. They have been away from each other too long and Pa melts at Ma's touch, just like I do when I need her when I am hurt and crying. They hold each other until Nanny and Pop interrupt the moment, struggling through the front door with their luggage.

Pa drops Ma's hand and leaves her struggling with her tears. He goes to help the grandparents, who are dragging their belongings along the wooden floor. Pa wipes his eyes quickly and points the way to the small bedroom at the front of the house where Nanny and Pop will sleep.

As Nanny opens the door of their room that has been closed during the hot day, the gush of heat inside pours out all over her. Nanny turns to Pa and says, "O my, is this what it is always like?"

She turns towards Pop. "Was it such a good idea coming to this God-forsaken desert land?"

I feel their tensions rise as Pa escapes off to organise warm water for our baths as Ma has asked him to. I follow him and when I get to the outside wash shed behind the house, I see that a small tin tub is set up for us. Pa is pouring hot water from the fire into it.

"Whoever gets in first has the hottest and cleanest water," Pa yells as he cools the hot water with some cold water. "Only one of you at a time," Pa yells again as all of us are now pushing and shoving each other to try to climb in first. It is conceded that it is my turn to have the clean water as I arrived first.

"The water doesn't want to lather Pa!" I call to him.

He replies, "It is bore water and the soap that is made here on the farm doesn't lather in it, but it cleans us." He reassures us and stays to safeguard our wild activities of bathing until all of us are clean. To our surprise, there is only a little of the cold, filthy water left in the tub after we use many bathtubs full of water. As we leave, we notice that the shed is drenched with most of the water splashed up the walls and all over the floor.

Pa then goes to help light the kitchen fire for Ma so she can prepare the evening meal. In no time, Ma and Nanny have a meal ready for the oven. The heat from the oven fills the room.

The two of them are loudly complaining. Ma says to Pa, "The hot air is rising and is ricocheting through all the rooms. It is almost unbearable to be inside." Ma runs to get wet cloths to wrap around their necks as they struggle to cook in the hot kitchen.

We thank them for their efforts when we eat everything they have cooked. The whole family is so grateful that we can eat fresh meat and vegetables grown on the farm. As we finish off the kitchen chores together for the night, Ma and Pa hug again and Pa tells us in his own way, "We will make a new home together here."

It is our bedtime, and we are excited to be sleeping our first night in our new home. "Hana, this is your bed, which you will share with Mara," Pa says. He points to the bed near the window at the far end of the large veranda at the back of the house. It has been converted into a bedroom for all the children. Pa continues, "The bedroom contains enough bedding to rest all of you exhausted sea-faring travellers. Of course, it is shared beds as it was in the homeland, and the littlest one will sleep in a small bed beside Ma and me in our separate bedroom."

Our first night in beds with mosquito nets hung over us feels very strange for me. But I realise why the nets are over the beds when a thousand mosquitos attack me the moment that I put a foot outside the net. The most dreadful trouble comes when I try to catch the mosquitos that get caught in the net with me. "Pa, come and get the mosquitoes inside my net!" I keep screaming until Pa comes. Now I feel tensions rise in me.

Days and weeks pass, and we are getting used to finding snakes, spiders, hundreds of insects that cover the lights at night, and wild animals that hop on their back legs. We learn quickly that we know very little of this country's ways.

Pa teaches us constantly. "You need to be careful in your wanderings around the farm. Watch where you are putting your feet when walking around outside. There could be snakes under any rock and slithering in the grasses. You will learn each day holds another lesson for you on how to survive in this land."

We have all been given our daily chores of carrying water to the house from the bore, chopping wood and gathering kindling for the fires, feeding the chickens, and gathering their eggs, milking the house cows, and picking the vegetables for the meals. Pa tells us sternly, "All the chores need be done each day before going to school, and when you arrive home in the afternoons."

Ma, Nanny, and Mara decide to travel to the closest town for supplies as soon as it is possible. A few days later, they leave early for this full day trip to collect any mail and food, and to scour the town for cool materials to make outfits for all of us.

Pa and Pop work hard running the farm, clipping the sheep for wool, and killing sheep for meat to sell, as well as meat for the workers, managers, and owners. Ma and Mara have also been hired as cooks and cleaners for the many workers on the farm. Nanny takes on the main running of the family's home and Pop helps Pa on the farm.

By the end of six months, we have struggled to barely adjust to the climate. Ma keeps telling us, "We are all waiting for a cool autumn as in the old country, and hoping for the cold of winter to come because we know how to cope with the cold."

However, we all soon realise there is hardly an autumn like we knew in the homeland. In Australia, it is still hot until the middle of the year. Then overnight, Ma complains, "This winter has hit us like an icy blast from the Antarctic. One day, it is hot and the next it is freezing cold."

Winter too is hard for Ma, Nanny, and Mara who are now busy spinning the scraps of sheep's wool from the last shearing season to make new jumpers and more blankets to keep us all warm.

As more time passes, I know I am growing as wild as the wind with a temperament to match. I love riding the horses and training them, or maybe them training me. I feel my long auburn hair flowing behind me when I ride across the dry, open plains with dust covering my skin and clothes. I love being with all the children on the farm, and with my brothers and sisters.

We have also become popular with the local children, and I run with them into the mischief that only we can conjure up together. Our spare time is spent wandering the empty riverbeds that are waiting for the spring rains to come again after winter.

We follow along the outstretched winding channels cut by the raging floods of the previous years, and I become lost in my imaginings. We learn every turn and bend in the banks of the river and greet every wild animal we meet. I love becoming one with the land. The local children and I lose ourselves in nature, and in the neighbours' friendships that will last a lifetime. I feel I am home in my new land.

After a freezing winter, the spring floods do come and wash away our footprints from the river and creek beds. We are cut off from the rest of the community as the water flood the plains. The house has been built on high stilts, especially for the rainy seasons. Pa tells us to take all our belongings from under the house and put them on the verandas. The wide-open verandas that encircle the house become our playground until the water subsides. Pa explains to us, "Still the underground water supply is replenished, and the rivers will nourish the paddocks for the next season."

Looking back during those first months in our new land, the weather was hard for all of us to cope with. It took us, as new Australians, beyond our limit as we realised the climate could be extreme. It showed us that it could be extremely hot and extremely cold. We could have anything from extreme drought to extreme floods in the summer and into winter, with not much variation in between.

Our first Australian Christmas approaches as summer arrives again. "It is not going to be a white Christmas this year," Ma tells us.

"How do we celebrate Christmas here then?" I ask Ma.

"We will have to make new Christmas traditions, Hana. You can all let your wild imaginings create other ways to celebrate Christmas." And our task begins.

We are all left doubting if it is good to change Christmas too much. All we are really worried about, though, is if Father Christmas is going be able to find us at the bottom of the world. I ask Ma and she reassures all of us. "Although it is a long trip to Australia, Father Christmas will make the journey and will bring you all gifts."

Pa and Pop go out into the bush to cut a large spindly pine tree for a Christmas tree for the family room. Each night, all of us children sit together and make decorations from coloured paper and tinsel Ma and Mara bought at the shops in town. We put gumnuts and wattle flowers on branches that we have collected to make into wreathes.

Ma, Mara, and Nanny set about making traditional fruitcakes and puddings. Pa and Pop kill enough lambs for a traditional Christmas roast dinner for all the workers as well as for us. They manage to kill and cook a couple of chickens as well. Presents are bought or handmade and we wrap them in special paper. We stack them under the tree until all we must do is wait to see if Father Christmas has been in the morning. Squeals of delight awaken everyone as the sun comes up on our first Christmas morning in our new home.

I awaken immersed in my soul's history, as I stumble out of bed the next morning as Asina. I'm overcome by vivid recollections of what seems to me to be my real life. I carry the vision internally as I set about preparing for my Christmas day with the family. During my chores of the day, my mind is full of the experiences of my past.

In the coming days, I come to believe I have travelled with my soul back in time to over a hundred earth years ago to become immersed in a family I have not known before. I know I have also travelled back to the great meeting of souls that took place nearly two centuries ago.

Curiously I ask Spirit, "Are these two happenings synchronistic?" I hear no answer, but I am left with the feeling that the two events I'm experiencing are aligned. I am unable to let the concept of my own participation in them leave me. I reverberate with the knowledge that my soul has visited and lived in the events of the past as Hana. I question Spirit, "Was I Hana in another lifetime? Are these souls my ancestors? Is this why my soul again participated within the conclave of souls?"

The souls of Hana and her family are becoming so close to me. I find myself attached to them on the earth and bonded to their souls

27

in heaven. I am so anxious to know what happened to each of them and their descendants. I contemplate the thoughts, *Are they part of the agreement made at the assembly of the gentling souls? Are they the first arrivals of the gentling souls?* I am mesmerised by these thoughts.

Chapter 5

RESEARCH BEGINS

The notion of a night of travelling in the soul state fascinates me. The familiarity of the metaphysical circumstances entices me to search for more of my family history through my paternal relatives. I want to find out who these people are and to discover if they are connected to the summoning of the conclave of souls. Do they consent to the submission and agreement achieved at the monumental gathering?

I seek answers about my paternal ancestors from my relatives and find they did emigrate to Australia over a hundred years ago. My great grandmother was called Hana and was a child when she arrived, as I anticipated. They landed near a seaport not too far away from where I now live, and they too eventually resided in the same region.

I am excited to be an intrinsic part of Hana's story and I want to know more of Hana's private life. I want to learn of the continuation of Hana's lineage throughout the years that lead up to my birth. I find out that she married another emigrant from the homeland named Clarrie. I want to meet Hana's husband Clarrie and I want to know of his genealogy. I want to be more informed of her children's lives and the lives of their children. Through her children, I want to become familiar with the years following Hana's departure from earth to find the connection to the present generation.

As I wait for my next journey with my heavenly companion, an interruption to my family's peace comes to us in the form of the pending departure of my brother to the spirit world. My brother only arrived back in my life weeks before Nettie, my youngest daughter, returned to heaven. His arrival synchronized with her illness.

His unexpected phone call to me, just to catch up after many years of no contact with each other, came as a complete surprise to me. I felt awkward as he told me first of his friend who was dying of cancer. He was suffering grief over losing a dear friend, and he obviously needed to tell someone by turning to me in his pain. Maybe he realised he had let our relationship fade almost into non-existence.

He had deliberately cut me out of his life after he remarried someone who he was not willing to share with me. I sat and listened to him and commiserated with him. It had been years since I had talked to him, but it felt like I had just talked to him yesterday. There was no gap between us; it had disappeared. I held no grudges, and I reached out to him in his time of need. After he had spoken, I asked him if he wanted to know of my plight. "Yes, of course," he replied.

I told him my daughter was dying of cancer too. He was shocked as his daughter from his first marriage was born only weeks before my daughter. We had been together then and he knew my daughter well. It was another moment of pain for him and reconciliation for us both.

After his initial phone call, he visited me often as Nettie prepared to leave. We became close during the months ahead. He stood by me as my daughter was lifted into the ambulance for her last trip to hospital. She didn't come home again.

My soul connects to him now as he is preparing for his own departure. He is in much pain and tells of his desire to leave. I cannot visit him in hospital due to COVID restrictions. On the morning he departs, our souls unite eternally.

Now I realise that throughout his earthly life, he maintained his position as a supporter of his sister, albeit distant. His leaving now has made me question his role in the conclave in which my family of souls participated. Was he truly a companion soul? I feel so emotional and in awe of his chosen duty in the family.

Time seems to move slowly after his leaving, and in my soulful and sorrowful state during the space between awake and asleep, I long to return to my soul's realm to be with my celestial companions once more.

This journey comes soon enough. When I arrive, I find that Hana's aunt Mara has met a young lad who works as a shearer on the farm. During this visit, I watch the couple become close friends and spend as much time as they can together when the shearing season is over.

I notice that I too am growing into a young woman, and I am also getting attention from the young male farm hands. Currently, I spend most of my days outdoors working the farm. I love the excitement of the land and the animals, and I know I am as good as any of the blokes with the sheep, especially in rounding them up on the large farm horses that love the chase with the dogs.

Ma watches me closely and is very aware of my future needs even if I am not at Mara's point in my life. Ma often tells me, "Hana, it won't be long before you will be finished at the rural school and need to go to the city for further education. You need to start to become more feminine and cultured." I teasingly laugh back at her remarks.

Very soon, the day arrives when Mara is ready to leave the family. I am chosen to be a bridesmaid for her wedding, which is to be held at the farm. I am dressed in "ladylike" finery as I watch them say their vows to each other. Mara leaves with her new husband in their carriage we all helped prepare for them, decorating it with ribbons, flowers, and strings of tin cans.

They leave the family and the farm to start a new life together renting a small house and working in the city. I now must become more help at home for Ma and Nanny, which means spending most of my time indoors. I cringe and complain, but I do as I am told.

Another year passes and I finish school. I head to the city to complete my education. Like Mara, I am glad to pass down my chores to my younger siblings and begin a city life as a secondary school student.

Ma and Pa send me to board with Mara, but even after a year away, I still suffer homesickness for the dusty, vast land. Mara soon has a little one and I am excited to have a little cousin to watch over. I miss my youngest sibling, who was born after we arrived in Australia.

The years at school slip by quickly. Soon, I take up studies to become a schoolteacher while teaching at a primary school in the city. By now, I have two little cousins. I have moved into a boarding house, made many friends, and become accustomed to city life.

It is here that I meet a young man who has only recently arrived in Australia from our homeland. Clarrie is five years older than I am and is living in the boarding house with his brother. They are both homesick for their family. They suffer from lack of nutrition and the effects of a long journey by sea.

There seems to be an immediate attraction to each other, either from our mutual connection to the homeland or because of our adventurous qualities and the rigorous journeys to a new land. Whatever it is, I take great pleasure interacting with Clarrie and showing him the ways of new Australians.

Clarrie tells me they have come from a county bordering our family's county. It also suffered severe devastation with diseased crops. He tells us, "It is taking years to rejuvenate the land, so we decided to leave to start again."

I ask him about his family. "My older brother Paddy and I are the only children in the family. Mammie died when I was twelve

32

and Pa remarried soon after she died. We just didn't fit in anymore. The two of us tried to get Pa to come with us but he didn't want to immigrate, so we had to leave him behind." Clarrie's face saddens as he lowers his head with tears in his eyes and says, "There was no future for Paddy and me in our homeland."

I seek work for them on the farm to help them both out. I keep in touch with Clarrie as they both recover from malnutrition and its related illnesses while earning a living and working on the farm. When I am at the farm, I spend my time with Clarrie. I realise he and Paddy have brought the homeland tradition of "having a pint or two every now and then" with them.

Before long, Paddy meets, falls in love with, and marries a girl from town. They move into town to live and work. My relationship with Clarrie develops slowly, as I only see him during the holidays. After completing my studies, I find a teaching position back in my country town at the local school, which has extended since I was there as a student. Excitedly, I now become one of two teachers at the school.

My family has been in Australia nearly ten years and we have become more accustomed to the country. Clarrie and I decide to marry, and great celebrations are being planned. Ma, Nanny, and I travel to the city to choose materials for my bridal gown, and for my bridesmaids' gowns. I choose white silk and lace for my gown, and for the girls' gowns, I choose a pale pink silk. For my veil, I choose white tulle with lily of the valley flowers for a head piece.

Relieved with her purchases, Ma sighs. "We will go back another day to choose colours and materials for mine and Nanny's outfits, and also the men's outfits." She further explains, "Although we have started six months before the wedding date, there is so much to accomplish."

For the first time in my life, I am excited and happy to create and wear beautiful finery suitable for a lady. The house has been turned into a sewing machinists' haven, with paper patterns, materials, cottons, zips, buttons, pins, scissors and ribbons and bows adorning the huge loungeroom and every other spare room. Sewing commences and stress reigns.

When the sewing is almost complete, invitations, decorations, and food all need to be planned and the loungeroom must be turned back into a reception area. My brothers are given instructions by the women to move this piece of furniture here and move that piece there.

As directed, Pa, Pop, and Clarrie oversee the management of killing enough beef, lambs, and chickens for the wedding feast. The closer the day comes, the more my anticipation grows that everything and everyone is going to be ready for the final rehearsal. I am ready for the marriage to take place.

Early in the morning of my wedding day, I slip quickly out of bed and stand staring at the sunrise over the wide-open downs. I am reminded of the day I left my homeland. Somehow it all seems familiar. Maybe it is, as once again, today is the finality of not living in my family home any more as a child. This morning too will be placed deep within my memories.

The wedding day opens into a glorious sunny, spring Saturday, not quite hot enough to be unbearable. All scurry around fixing food, clothes, and carriages to get us to town before the wedding at noon. All horse-drawn carriages and buggies are ready with their decorations and their passengers. However, at this moment, mine is still empty.

Pa is waiting at the closed-in bridal carriage for me to arrive so we can all leave together in a wedding procession. His facial expression when he sees that I am wearing my riding boots under my silk gown is hilarious. "You're not wearing those boots, Hana," he yells at me.

"No Pa!" I yell back laughing. "I have my silk slippers in my bag to put on at the church. I don't want them to get them dirty."

"I wouldn't put it past you Hana, I am surprised you have washed up as pretty as you have."

Pa travels with me in the bridal carriage and I get teary sitting beside my father for the last time. I will soon be a married woman and no longer his little girl. A tear drops on my cheek. He notices my emotion and holds my hand with his thick, coarse hand. Another moment in time I will never forget.

We arrive at the church and the pleasantries begin. Inside the church lined with flowers and candles, all seems to be culminating into a grand day for Clarrie and me. We take our vows in front of a packed church and as I kneel before the altar, I feel the presence of a heavenly entourage all around us. I can feel the divine approval of our union.

After the ceremony, and by the time we arrive back at the farm, everyone has relaxed and is ready for a long night of food, drink, dancing, and celebration. Clarrie and I leave somewhere just before midnight and head back to our rented house in town. We look at each other and realise we have just become husband and wife. After crawling out of my beautiful dress, I settle down on my bed to wait for Clarrie to finish stabling the horses, but my eyes close heavily for the first time today and I fall into a deep sleep.

As I leave Hana again, I am becoming more aware that the conclave of souls and my experiences as Hana in the continuing tale of her life are connected. The sun rises as I awaken from my transcendental travels, and again, I am alone in my own bed feeling sorry for Clarrie of long ago. After this journey, I am beginning to believe that Clarrie, due to his deprived past, could be the first gentling soul coming into my family.

Chapter 6

CLARRIE AND HANA

Now I need to make some inquiries to find the beginnings of Clarrie's life. Who were his parents? Who were their parents? Is there any inkling of gentling souls beginning along his side of the family? Or down Hana's line? Where do the signs of gentling souls first appear?

With all the questions floating around in my head, I seek any knowledge of my paternal lineage from my sister, who is in contact with paternal cousins. We sift through memories and written information from cousins who have visited the homeland and followed the trail of Hana, and from our great grandmother's family.

It takes some phone calls and long visits to the paternal side of my family to get any responses to my enormous list of questions. I am so excited when I realise one cousin has already searched for Hana and offers us her results.

I examine my cousin's findings and I conclude that Hana's paternal grandparents, who she left behind to emigrate to Australia, did live on in the homeland. Hana did indeed come with her parents, aunt, and maternal grandparents back in the mid-1800s.

I also find my paternal great grandfather Clarrie's history. I find that the beginning of the gentling souls' impairment may have started in his family and continued down our line when he married Hana.

As my curiosity is now ignited, we decide to meet up with the paternal side of the family again. I sit for hours and listen as the verbal stories emerge, especially that of Clarrie's heritage as it was handed down through the generations and is unfolding before me while I take notes.

"Back in the early 1800s, your great-great grandparents met as young children living and going to school in the district next to the place where you originated. Mary and Thos were destined to be together as they spent their young lives constantly in each other's company. They were around the same age and lived paupers' lives on the same farm with their labourer parents. Although Thos ran with the wild boys, he protected Mary from their tormenting behaviours and rivalry.

The pair became trusted friends early in life. No one was surprised when they married and continued their parents' way of life on the landlord's farm. They lived contentedly as a couple in a little worker's cottage on the farm and soon had their first child, Anne. Thos and Mary were both about twenty-one years of age when Mary gave birth to Anne. Thos worked hard for a living and was proud of his little family.

However, Mary fared poorly and barely recovered from the birth of her child. The next winter, she died of pneumonia, leaving her baby motherless. Anne was wretchedly undernourished and failing to thrive when Mary's mother Jane took her each day for Thos so he could work. Jane struggled working and maintaining her home and family as well as cooking and keeping the little cottage for Thos and Anne clean.

However, it seemed to Jane that Thos was falling deeper into despair since his Mary's death. The time soon came when he left Anne with Jane permanently. Without the baby, Thos found his way to the tavern nightly and was seen each morning waking in the streets after a night of heavy drinking. Eventually, Thos fled his responsibilities and difficulties. He was last heard of years later by travellers who said he was living in another county. He had remarried. He never came back for Anne.

Little Anne always remained sickly. She grew into a quiet young girl and young woman who knew no other life but hard work on the farm with her grandparents. It was here that she met Pat, a young lad who worked on the farm as well. They became close friends. They married soon after and moved into the same little cottage where Anne's mother and father started their life together.

A year later, their first son Paddy was born. However, because of Anne's poor health, they waited three years before she had their second son, Clarrie. After a life of continued declining health, Anne passed at the age of thirty-three when Paddy was fifteen and Clarrie was only twelve. Their father Pat and his boys did their best to cope without Anne, but none of them were surviving her death or the hardship of the land. Pat remarried and tried his best to incorporate the boys into a new family, but they felt alienated and grew distant. They began getting into trouble around the town.

At that time, there was still little hope of a future in Ireland for young people, and most of the inhabitants were immigrating to distant lands seeking better lives. Paddy and Clarrie begged their father to come with them to Australia, but he refused and stayed on in his home. Anne and Pat's two boys arrived in Australia when Paddy was twenty-three and Clarrie was twenty years old."

After listening to the tale of the two young men, I now know back as far as our great-great grandparents, Clarrie's grandparents. I feel so heartbroken for Anne losing her mother so young, never knowing her father, and for Paddy's and Clarrie's loss of Anne, their mother, when they were so young. What a start to a new life in Australia for the two young men who had to leave their father behind as well as their mother at rest at home.

I'm finally alone with the pieces of the two men's story to process. I have papers and notes to myself spread all over the floor. I am still learning more of Hana's early life with Clarrie, and how he coped with his losses as he came to terms with all he had already lived and left behind.

I need to try to get some sleep tonight, but my mind is freely setting its own course. I can't seem to stop the process of travelling. The next thing I know, I am Hana. I have Clarrie beside me as we wake up in the morning after our wedding. The shreds of information I have just gathered are fading away as I reencounter my new husband. This morning, we will start making our family home in our little town. We are happy with the decision that Clarrie will work in town while I continue teaching there.

During the weekends and my regular school holidays, we decide to roam the countryside together, to get to know other areas we have only been told about. On our first opportunity to travel, we choose to visit the small bayside town where we first arrived with its wide sandy beaches and sheltered surf.

When we first stepped onto the pier in the little bay, we experienced a land so different from the homeland. Today, Clarrie and I walk for hours along the wide beaches, talking together of our individual experiences of living in Ireland and of leaving her behind. We talk about how I came with my family as a child, and how Clarrie had more recently arrived with his brother after their long journey together to a new country. We stop and look at where we are now standing, together in our new country. We embrace tightly as if finding each other was a miracle. We promise each other, "We will always be together."

We stand on the foreshore and gaze out to the horizon from whence we came. As we turn to each other, we agree when I say, "Let's make this place always a part of our lives. We can rent a room in one of the boarding houses here each year for our annual holidays." The agreement is sealed with a kiss.

We decorate our little home with our wedding gifts. Finally, I am at peace being alone with Clarrie. All is going so well for us, and we are so happy. Clarrie seems to be getting well and his homesickness is dissipating, although he still seems anxious and drinks to subside his moods. I often wonder if his anxious drinking is in his nature, or if it is his reaction to his troublesome life so far. Probably a bit of both, I presume.

A year or two passes and we decide that I will give up teaching for a while so we can have a baby. Clarrie will bring in the only income. We finally have our first child. We are so happy with our little son. He is a lively little boy—a bit like his mother, with a crop of auburn hair and a personality to match. He is now up and following his Pa and Grandpa everywhere. By this time, Nanny and Pop have both journeyed home to Jesus, and Ma and Pa have only one child at school in town. They decide to move to town and live close to us.

When little Tommy is old enough for me to go back to teaching, Ma watches her grandchild. Life becomes normal for us at home and at work. About a year later, our little Tommy becomes extremely sick with a fever. I take leave and stay home with him until he seems to be recuperating. Before I can go back to teaching, he takes a turn for the worse and unexpectedly he returns to heaven. Both Clarrie and I are beyond heartbroken.

Ma and Pa support us as they know the pangs of losing a child, having lost a little one while living in their homeland. The whole family suffers the loss. We immerse ourselves in silence and work, and Clarrie and I seem to be silent in our own company. Soon after, we hear from Clarrie's stepmother that his father Pat had passed. Both deaths are hard on both of us, but more so on Clarrie, as the homeland has now become void of immediate family for the two brothers.

A year passes and I ask Clarrie if we could have another child and he agrees. Soon we have our little girl. She brings great joy to all of us as a couple and to the wider family. Our family grows with happiness. We continue to have more children all two to three years apart, until we have our five little girls interspersed between our three little boys in our family. We survive the loss of Tommy, but we still miss him. I know Clarrie and Paddy feel like orphans with both parents now deep within the land of their births.

As our children grow, I notice our girls are quieter and more reserved than I ever was and still am. They are extremely anxious, and I find them sensitive in their emotions. The girls find it difficult to learn and to socialise without great effort. The boys are boisterous and outgoing and thrive on any school or outdoor activities. As they all reach school age, I see them with their friends and I become very aware of their differences, especially in the temperaments between our boys and our girls.

I know all my children are good students. They try hard at their work and achieve pleasing results. They are well behaved, but still the girls learn slowly, are socially awkward, and uncoordinated when they try to run. They try hard to keep their emotions under control. Consequently, they are uncomfortable in school and social situations. They are clumsy at play, unlike the boys, who seem to gallivant through their schoolwork and play.

The girls are overly emotional at home with their siblings. Interactions can explode into tears and tantrums without much provocation. Of course, the boys tease their sisters as boys do, and I feel I am always shielding the girls against their brothers.

Chapter 7

A LITTLE DIFFERENT

I know that it is inappropriate to talk about learning difficulties or anxieties among family and especially not among friends or medical professionals. I try to talk to Clarrie, but he will have none of it, saying to me, "They are all right. They are just girls."

I reply sternly, "How would you know? You've never had sisters." The argument could go on and on.

Clarrie seems to be missing from our family home more these days. He is either working or inebriated most of the time at home. He tells me he drinks to ease the pain and to calm his nerves as he is suffering from muscle strain from the hard work. Gradually, I am becoming his caregiver.

I realise that I can't explain my suspicions about the difference in my girls to anyone else other than Ma. I talk to her constantly about what is deep in my soul. "Ma, I just know there is something amiss," I tell my mother.

Ma knows what I am talking about as she helps me with the children constantly and consoles me with her words. "You are raising your girls beautifully. They are loved by others for their kindness and gentleness, and although they shy away from activities, they will survive."

I know there is disparity between my girls and the other girls I have taught. I talk to my mother again about the girls. "Ma, I don't know what is wrong with my girls. I don't remember being so awkward and unsocial at school and so unwilling to play outside. Was I the same as the girls?"

Ma tells me, "No, you were always outdoors. Don't worry Hana—they are just a little different. They'll be all right."

"But Ma, Mara's girls are not like my girls."

"No, I agree, they are not, but your girls are just as they are. Nothing can be done, other than learning what they need and trying to give them all they need." Ma acknowledges my dilemma and supports my concerns. As Ma tells me, "They just suffer from nerves. They are just a little different." I feel so alone and drained. I tell no one else of my family issues.

"But Ma, it is hard for me to adjust to the townsfolk, particularly at school, in church, or at other public places. Impairments are difficult for others to accept. The pitying sighs I endure from those who are supposed to be my friends unravel me when I am exhausted."

"I know Hana, but you are a very strong personality and can brace yourself to stand up for your girls," Ma assures me.

"Yes, I will persevere in trying to socialise the girls through others' oppositions," I reply. "I will teach them, as young adults, to gently become accustomed to the township's opposition and I will continue to present them as well-dressed and well-mannered citizens in society."

Still, I am so frustrated with no answers. "Being a little different is never talked about, Ma. I have become very dependent on your help, especially with the girls." Ma nods solemnly.

Life moves on and the children are developing slowly in their lives in their own ways when Ma, my beautiful mother, must let go of life. In her last hours of such an exceptional life, I sit with her, and we only talk of love.

"Ma, you have been so brave to come to this land and raise us up to become fine citizens of our new country. Your love has spread through this family like a river flowing through our dry land. You have nourished love and family as your only intention for your life. Thank you for the power of your love."

Tears trickle from her aged eyes as she whispers, "I love you!" She returns home to heaven and leaves all of us—her children and her grandchildren—on our own to grow the family in the new land. She is now with both Pa and Mara, who have been gone for some time.

I now feel on my own with no support in raising the girls. It is up to me now to support the children and for them to help me around the house with the chores. I struggle with the girls, and I pray for their success.

During my losses, I become close to Saint Anthony. I have always admired the picture of him hanging above Ma's bed. I now seek his advice about how to help my girls as I place his painting above my own bed.

After this visit, I stare at the picture of Saint Anthony above my bed as I straighten the bedding the next morning after travelling. I am overwhelmed that this image belonged to Hana, my great grandmother, who I believe I have now met and embody on my visits.

This time, I return full of concerns for Hana. How did she cope with her problems? How did her girls turn out? What is happening in the family of girls? Why only the girls?

My lineage is becoming an enormous field of knowledge for me to begin to comprehend. I am beginning to see likenesses in my own generation to that of Hana's generation. It is becoming unnerving for me to grasp the specific genetic attributes that exist in the generations. *What does all this mean?* I contemplate answers as next I wait to visit my ancestors.

The next day, I remember the story told to me as I received the painting of Saint Anthony of Padua. My paternal cousin gave the painting to me many years ago, long after her mother, my paternal aunt, passed.

My cousin told me, "One day, I was clearing out my storage room and I came across this painting of my mother's. I remembered there was an adage in the family about you, Asina, and my mother. I was always told, 'Your mother will never be dead as long as Asina is alive!'

"I remembered that you were attached to my mother, and I want to give the painting to you. I have packed up the painting in the old, tattered paper in which it was stored after she left, thinking you may like to see the age of the wrapping," she said, handing me the huge painting.

Momentarily, I am stunned, as I have always been aware I resembled my paternal aunt in many ways. I vaguely remember being told as a child that I was like her. These ancient familial words ignited my memory of my aunt in my heart and mind, and I received the painting graciously.

I removed the aged paper gently. It crinkled at my touch as I slowly unwrapped the sepia painting. Memories of it hanging over my aunt's bed came flooding back to me. It felt like a gift coming to me through the ages. I placed the painting above my bed as it has always been above the beds of the women in my paternal lineage: Hana's grandmother, Hana's mother, Hana, my paternal grandmother, her daughter, and now me, Asina. *'Six generations!'*

I consider the enormity of the number of years Saint Anthony has been the patron saint of my paternal family. I try to remember what I was told by my aunt about the life of Saint Anthony. I remember she wrote a prayer to Saint Anthony on a beautiful card and gave it to me when I was young and full of doubt and anxieties. I still have the card to this day.

All I know of Anthony is that his family originated in Portugal. My maternal grandmother was born on a south Atlantic island belonging to Portugal. Anthony had undying love for Jesus and devotion to the poor and sick. I realise I somewhat resonate with his qualities.

I treasure the painting above my head and the enormous spiritual connection I have with the child Jesus, who Saint Anthony is holding in the picture. The image depicts Jesus stepping out of the Bible Anthony is holding and becoming alive for him, and for me.

There is safety in knowing this painting has come from the generations I have recently encountered. I believe Anthony has a message to tell me. I believe it is connected to the conclave of souls I have attended with my heavenly companion.

I also reflect on my time with my aunt, who I became close to when I came to live with my biological parents when my grandmother Ezara became ill. Back then, I refused to walk to school on my own when I first arrived at my biological parents' home. It was a forty-minute walk on my own each way.

I remember I became hysterical one morning and refused to go to school when my friend was not going to walk that day. I was mortified that there was no one to walk with me, so I ran to my aunt who lived close by and she offered to walk with me. After that day, we became close companions and we regularly walked together. We were very alike, which seems to be our attraction to each other.

During this time, I would sometimes stay on at her home after school and became close to my cousins. The middle of the three children seemed different, but I was not bothered by his sudden emotional outbursts, his struggle to speak, and his clumsy body. I grew to love him just as one of my cousins and spent numerous visits with him. I felt at home in their family. I knew I was understood and protected.

It was my aunt who visited me in one of my more recent connections to the spiritual realm. She came into my home office where I was working, came up close to me, and stood beside me. I said to her, "You are dead, aren't you?" She laughed. My aunt had passed years earlier and now I was meeting her in spirit accompanied by a huge figure.

Referring to the eight-foot-tall figure standing beside her, I asked, "Is this your caregiver? I know you were sick. Are you still in need of a caregiver?" She laughed again.

"What are you doing here?" I asked, confused. "You came up my driveway at such a great speed and screeched to a halt just before you hit the stump of the house. I thought you were going to crash into the house. You frightened me." She did not reply. If she only wanted to get my attention, she had succeeded.

I got up from my desk and walked with her and her tall companion outside to the utility they had just exited. I was shocked when I saw a small child in the back tray, hanging tightly onto the side of the vehicle. "Hello," I said quietly, as I reached out to pick the child up. I turned to my aunt and asked, "What is happening? Who is this child on its own in the back of the ute? That was so dangerous. This feels like one of my children, but I don't know which one!" I received no answer from my aunt.

Carrying the child from the open tray of the truck, I looked around and saw my aunt and her tall companion sitting on the outdoor bench in my garden, talking with my biological mother, who was still living on earth at that time. I am confused and I am left standing there holding the child as my aunt and her caregiver disappear.

The meeting always bothered me as I moved forward with my life. It wasn't until I was at Nettie's funeral that I told the story of my aunt's visit to her daughter, my cousin, who gave me the picture of Saint Anthony. In retelling the story to my cousin, I realised her mother had come to prepare me for the death of my daughter Nettie.

This was my own child I took from the back tray of the truck. Her arrival certainly startled me, as it was a warning of the pending death of my child. She showed me she was in danger.

We both stopped the conversation realising that my aunt would certainly come to support and prepare me and walk with me through my sorrow as she walked with me to school. I know she once again protected me. I always feel great gratitude and love for my gentle aunt.

I am beginning to believe the souls who are entering the earth through my great grandmother Hana and my great grandfather Clarrie are the first generation of the gentling souls. I cannot tell anyone of my perspective, but this generation interests me even more because it is the beginning of the generation of my paternal grandmother.

Chapter 8

ASINA

Each day, I build more confidence and curiosity to keep searching for my family's ancestors. Soon, I am invited to travel the ethers again with my companion to reach the early generations of my family. I know that the arrival in the past this time will be important for me. This time, I will be able to experience the early development of my own generation and to experience their responses and adjustments to any impairment that may occur.

When I arrive this time as Hana, I instantly feel I am becoming more aware of the growing needs of the girls. I choose to give hours of support to them and dote on them as they display erratic emotional behaviours that can upend the family's serenity.

As the girls reach their early teens, I am convinced that there is some form of impairment flowing through my family, especially through the girls. It is the first time in my family line that something like this has happened. I worry constantly and try to find answers as life becomes complicated.

As the girls grow into young women, I watch as they step out of my protection and make lives of their own and become competent with my help. My eldest girl does not marry and establishes a career in teaching. She finds personal relationships excruciatingly awkward and remains single. My next two daughters marry and choose not to have children.

My other two girls, Maud and the youngest Moira, eventually marry young men in the town. Maud and her husband give me my first grandson. I can see as I pick him up for the first time that there is something amiss. He is born with a distinctive impairment. I have not seen his extreme needs in my girls, and I choose not to say anything to Maud at this point. I know he is going to need special support and from that moment on I become their main assistance with the child.

It is the first time I am experiencing the impairment to this extent. I assume the complication is getting worse in this next generation. It is heartbreaking for me as I learn to become adept to my grandson's needs. Once again, it is difficult to immerse him in society. His mother tries, despite my disapproval, to make him a recluse at an early age.

My youngest daughter Moira, who has the same quiet and reserved characteristics as her sisters, remains close to the family and chooses to live close by us with her new husband, who is also a teacher. Moira becomes a willing homemaker. She supports Maud with her son and her two other children, who show no sign of any impairment. Moira is also my support.

Sometime later, Moira starts a family of her own with the birth of a little girl, who is full of vitality and reminds us of my own free spirit. I become inseparable from my grandchild as we share the same feisty traits with the same flowing red hair. She has no signs of any impairment, and we all feel relieved.

The family revels in her presence. Eighteen months later, Moira has twins, a pigeon pair, and as the first year passes, the three little children group together as one. All seems to be well. However, the little girl twin seems to be anxious and withdrawn, as Moira and Maud were as children. I am now a constant support for both my girls and their families.

During the twins' first winter, sickness strikes Moira's family and takes the three children down with high fevers. Moira says, "Mama, I am tired, and I think I am coming down with what the children have. I'm sorry for being such a nuisance to you, but could you stay tonight to help us with the children?"

I go home to get clothes. When I return, Moira is crying. "What is it?" I ask.

"Mama, he is getting worse, and we need to get him to hospital," Moira blurts out, picking up her little son. "Will you be okay with the girls?"

"Sure, you both get going and we will be fine here," I reassure her.

Sadly, the end of the week comes with the unexpected departure of their little boy. The couple are inconsolable, and his twin sister is bereft without him. I stay on to support the shattered family through their tragic loss. I remember my little boy and resonate too well with the pain of losing a child.

On awakening from this visit to Hana, I am left with a deep sorrow in my heart, understanding and knowing that my grandmother Moira suffered the loss of her son. This event has shaken me, for I too have given birth to a pigeon pair. Around the same age as her twins, my twin son also suffered the same disease and was hospitalised.

I relive my experience in sorrow but also relief. I remember I fought so hard to have his twin sister, who also was sick, put in the same hospital room as her brother, who was fretting for her through his illness. However, she was not as sick as my little boy. When I took her the next day for medical treatment, she was not admitted. After a tense week, I didn't lose my son. He survived with the modern medical treatments available. I feel so terribly saddened for my grandmother, who revisited her loss with me at the time of my son's sickness.

On my next visit as Hana, I find my daughter and her husband both strong, but they still need support to cope with their two little girls. I step back into caring for the children with Moira, and it is now I recognise my two granddaughters are so different from each other. The eldest is open and lively. The lone twin, who displays her grief by looking for her brother everywhere as if she is missing a part of herself, appears very emotional and even more sensitive and clingy than my girls were at this age.

Sometime later, Maud, Moira's sister, is about to give birth again. I rush off to support her as she has another son. From the beginning, he seems to have a slight impairment and is mildly affected—a similar effect as Maud and Moira, as well as the surviving twin, is showing. I am feeling overwhelmed as the family seems to be inundated with difficulties.

Life for Moira becomes a struggle after losing her baby. To break her grief of two long years, they decide they would like another child. Another son is born to the family. All seems well until he also presents as a quiet and reserved child as he gets older. He is very bright but emotionally clumsy. He keeps quiet most of the time, but Moira finds he can have emotional outbursts and takes them out on his sisters.

Their last child is born to the family years later with the same bubbly personality as their first child. Both these girls appear to have no impairment. They appear to be bookends to the family, as their mother comes to accept that the middle two children are the ones who display awkward symptoms as all my girls presented.

Their father Jed works hard teaching in the little local school, with his children attending classes there. He is home with the children more than Moira experienced her father Clarrie being home with her.

However, Jed's only son Gus is not living up to his expectations of being an active and outgoing son. Instead, Gus prefers to be on his own and retreats to quiet surrounds and indulges in study at school. He becomes a recluse in the family and spends time with his quiet mother in her gentle activities of sewing and cooking, as well as playing with the shy and lone twin.

When Gus finishes primary school, his father sends him to the city to board at a Christian boy's secondary school to develop both his scholastic and social skills. Gus psychologically struggles at the school, as he has little time to seclude himself as he is accustomed to doing. Instead, he uses study as a diversion from extra sport and socialising, and he attains excellent achievements in his work when he graduates.

Upon graduation, Gus turns seventeen and his father insists that Gus must stay in the city to find work. With his father's help, he finds a boarding house to live in and achieves a career in the railway. He mixes with older men who train him well for adulthood.

During this, Gus also meets Siroda at a church meeting and they begin to date. This is the very first girl Gus has been able to communicate with effectively. She is older than Gus, is an only child, and is somewhat a recluse herself living with her mother Ezara. They take their relationship very slowly and stretch their friendship to cover a few years for Gus to develop a career before they plan a wedding.

By this time, Moira's lone twin has met a local man. They spend a lot of time together and set plans to marry. They have their first child, who brings them great delight. Their second child comes soon after and he has a unique impairment from birth. Moira spends many hours supporting her daughter with her children while at the same time supporting me as I am preparing to leave this earth.

I am left thinking, *It is not easy for me to let go as I know the impairment has expanded in this generation. I have no idea how my children will cope without my support. I see the sadness in their eyes as I leave, and I cry for them all.*

From my abode in heaven, I watch the family adjust to my departure. It has only been six earthly months since Clarrie and

Paddy died just weeks apart. All the pioneers are home and together again.

In leaving the earth as Hana, I become witness to the day of my parting from the sacred realm of my soul. The day chosen for my funeral is the day my grandson Gus and Siroda have already chosen to marry. I watch as Moira decides to attend my funeral, instead of attending the wedding of her son. What a bittersweet day for them all to have to make a choice. I believe Gus will miss his mother terribly.

As a newly married couple, Gus and Siroda remain in the city where Gus came to study years ago. I try to communicate with Gus, and with Moira, but my attempts are to no avail. I can hear them, but they cannot hear me. While in the divine realm, I witness Gus and Siroda have a son who appears to have no genetic impairment from birth.

It is about this time World War 2 interferes in their lives and I watch as Gus leaves for battle overseas. I watch as Siroda is now living on her own in an upstairs flat while Gus is away. Her mother Ezara is living downstairs in her flat, supporting the new mother and her baby.

After Gus returns from war early with a medical discharge, I make my entrance on earth again. I become the second born into their family and I am named Asina. I am sensitive, emotional, and anxious, and I cry for constant reassurance. I am given to my maternal grandmother Ezara to raise from birth, as I am too difficult for my parents.

I live and grow with Ezara until mother and father have another two children in quick succession, and there is need to move out of the flat into a house. They take me with them against my will. For continued support for me, Ezara visits us weekly and takes me back home for the weekends.

Chapter 9

CHALLENGES

My life becomes chaotic with my mother and my father. I no longer have Ezara's understanding of my underlying symptoms of anxiety that have become exacerbated with the change of schools and houses, and the extra siblings. I am withdrawing socially at school, while struggling to learn in the huge classes of the era with up to ninety children in one classroom.

My life with my new sisters is exhausting. I have become their babysitter as Mother does not understand their needs and as Hana did not understand her daughters' needs. Mother does not cope well with their exceptional needs and innately I seem to understand them. I have become an integral part of their existence. They too are sensitive, anxious, and emotionally volatile with each other and within the family. Life becomes "normal" for all of us.

Mother takes the young ones to several medical professionals for assistance and is advised by all to just persist with their differences. She leaves without a diagnosis of any impairment, and she is only left with symptoms. It is a trying time for Mother as Father is never home, having established his own business where he is constantly working. He also begins to drink socially, but that soon becomes heavily to enhance his business opportunities as well as to calm his anxious behaviours.

My brother is the only son and delights in tormenting and teasing his sisters constantly because he receives negative feedback from us. Each day I seem to become the hitting bag for all the family to take swipes at, even though I can do nothing in return. I have become the scapegoat for everyone, including my parents. When I go home to live with Ezara each weekend and return each Sunday night, my position has weakened further in the family. I am an outsider.

When I do return to the family, my anxieties rise, I panic, and I burst into tears. I sustain emotional trauma after being belted for crying. I resist walking to school on my own, but Father is not available to drive me, and Mother doesn't drive. Again, I am treated with brutal beltings from my parents because I scream and resist.

I find school to be complicated because I cannot calm my nerves enough to concentrate. I seek my parents' help and support at home with my work, but there is none. If I do plead with my father, he will sit with me in a condescending manner and expect me to understand concepts on the first attempt. Even though I desperately seek my parents' attention in any way I can, I always come up short.

I wait to return to my mother each weekend and all holidays because she sits with me and creates and works with me. I have her and she has me. We are one. I learn very young I must survive the chaos for I will be able to come home each weekend.

I love to go to the church at school and sit with all the children in the weekly Mass celebrated just for the children and the teachers. It is here that I feel a oneness with everyone. We are also taught to visit the church in our breaks and speak to Jesus on our own. I love this time when I can wander into the church on my own and absorb the presence of the Divine. I fall in love with Jesus each time I visit him during my lunch break. I learn to withdraw into my soul with Jesus and Mary as a way of surviving home with my parents and siblings.

I fret for my real mother, my grandmother Ezara, who comforts me and accepts my anxieties and concerns. I can't wait for her to arrive each Tuesday or Wednesday and stay till Friday when my father takes us both home. I relax in bed with her again each night as she teaches me how to say the rosary. This is the life I absorb as my own, for I am home with my mother.

To further survive the chaos with the family, I withdraw into my room that I share with my younger sisters while I'm with them. However, this is when I am then accused of showing my sisters how to resist authority. When I am corrected, I am locked in my room on my own. Of course, in my rebellion, I open the window and climb out with no care that there is a long drop to the concrete path below. I have even ripped my hand open on the latch once or twice when I forgot to let go as I leaped to the ground. I have also landed on my knees on the fall many times, leaving me with bruises and gashes. Still, I run around to climb the back stairs and stand at the door to let Mother know that I freed myself, then mockingly run off to play outside.

My last sibling comes as I am finishing my last year in primary school and before I need to travel to secondary school in the city. Going to a different suburb closer to my mother, however, is excellent news for me as I can independently go to live with her whenever I want to.

I'm older now and more willing to become involved with my littlest sister. However, she also has sensitivities and anxious behaviours and withdraws from social interaction in the family and gatherings. Mother also takes her to many medical professionals and is given no further diagnosis as to what is causing her to be different from other children of her age. There are now all the girls in the family who present with impairments.

Mother just gets on with life and becomes silent about any troublesome issues with her children. Nothing is ever said other than it is all our fault that we are so difficult. However, I am the only one who is belted by both parents for being different.

Father comes home occasionally for dinner at night; other than that, we never see him. I can't blame Mother for being so distant and seemingly uncaring. She tries her utmost to maintain a home and family as best as she can, being an only child herself and with no understanding of any impairments.

Once in secondary school, I contact the family only when my mother Ezara suggests I need to go home for a while to keep everyone happy. I leave school at fifteen with only eighteen months until graduation and without asking or telling my parents or my mother. Father takes me into his workplace and gives me to his secretary to teach me some office education. According to him, "I'm not worth educating further as I am a girl, and I will only get married." Eventually, Father seeks a productive job for me, and I leave his employ.

I become more separated from the family. I am free to be with my mother now and can look after her as she gets older. By the time I am nineteen, I marry an office clerk who is working in the same company. He is then transferred to a country town, a four-hour drive away from my mother and the family. I am heartbroken and I quickly seek children of my own to fill the gap. Pregnancy is difficult with my emotional ailment, and I am sick throughout the nine months for each pregnancy. My Ezara did not live to see all my children, and it was easier to distance myself from the rest of the family after she was gone.

We decide to take our children on an adventurous alternate life and live far from society on an island in a sheltered bay in the Pacific. With a family house full of children, I become aware that some are a little different in temperament. However, I am used to being a little different myself and instinctively make allowances for their behaviour. I home school my children while running a small business where they learn about the business from the grass roots.

Years pass on the island, and it is here I am the happiest ever in my life. By teaching my children, I am relearning all over again the basics of the school curriculum that I missed as a child. I am feeling fulfilled as a wife, a mother, a teacher, a shop owner, and a farmer. I also continue my love for Christ and His mother. I share my relationship with God with each of my children by creating a holy sanctuary in a little room behind the kitchen where we gather for prayers each night.

When the children reach secondary schooling, we all decide we must leave our island home and re-enter society. We buy a large house in a beach town with good quality education. We also purchase a run-down business and redevelop it until it becomes a popular business in the township. My teens are now helping to run the business and learning more business skills that will take them further into higher education and employment.

The time comes soon enough for them all to leave home, and they all prepare for entering tertiary education in a distant city. Each of them qualifies for university. They take varying degrees to enhance their prospects of future employment. I also prepare and qualify for an applied science degree in psychology and enter university at the same time with them.

It is around this time that each of the young adults branch out into his or her own relationships. Next, we have all their weddings planned within the same year. I become involved in preparations amongst study and teaching and caring for my last child, who has a severe impairment.

Although no one in the family has been medically diagnosed, I can see that the symptoms are developing with each additional child. Still, we go on with life as if it doesn't matter as we have become accustomed to the discrepancies in the family.

It is not long after settling in the city that my children begin families of their own. The first grandson arrives and immediately we know there is an even more pronounced difference coming through in this generation. His body is also impaired with undeveloped movement as he grows. Medical professionals are brought in again and this time there are diagnoses of low muscle tone, difficulty with balance and speech, impaired vision, and an obvious development delay.

At this same time my younger sisters, who have always presented with difficulties, are also having children themselves with more severe symptoms. One of them seeks the support of medical professionals as well. The whole family are informed that testing has begun for a genetic disorder.

She has all her family tested as well as herself. She has been told that she tests positive for a genetic disorder causing the various symptoms presenting in effected children in the extended family, present and past. My other siblings undertake testing procedures immediately for themselves and their children.

Further information ricochets throughout my estranged family. It is found that the genetic anomaly began with our father, who has also tested positive to the disorder and is now suffering serious effects due to his age. We were told that the disorder has passed down via a discrepancy on the X chromosome through his mother Moira, our paternal grandmother.

With this distressing knowledge infiltrating my family, a whole new wave of confusion, fear, dread, and terror grips all my children as they realise that I too must be positive for the genetic disorder and passed it onto my children and now my grandchildren. From further information that is gathered and shared with the rest of the family, we are advised to be tested.

Chapter 10

GENETICS

Information given by the doctors on genetic disorders is shared among the family members. We are informed about genetic disorders inherited on the X chromosome.

We learn that a male has one X chromosome and one Y chromosome. A female inherits two X chromosomes.

A male inherits his X chromosome from his mother and inherits his Y chromosome from his father only.

A female inherits one of her X chromosomes from her mother and inherits the other X chromosome from her father.

A male passes his X chromosome to his all daughters and passes his Y chromosome to only his sons.

A female will pass only one of her X chromosomes to each child; it can be either the X chromosome from her mother *or* the X chromosome from her father.

A female has a 50 percent chance of passing a deficiency on her X chromosome to either a son *or* a daughter.

It is now evident that my father's genetic inheritance has come from an X chromosome from his mother Moira. His father has passed his Y chromosome to his son.

This being the case, my grandmother Moira has passed her deficient X chromosome, that she inherited either from her father or her mother, onto my father. We don't know which parent that is in this case. From the information I have gathered on Moira's father Clarrie, I suspect that the impairment may have come from her father. Then it passed to and affected all his and Hana's five daughters.

My father Gus must have passed his inheritance of his only X chromosome (the deficient X chromosome from his mother) on to all his daughters, including me.

This latest news delivered to us hits my family like a tsunami hits the coast, taking the very foundations from the land and leaving only devastation behind.

The young couples in my family who are beginning to have children are traumatised. We know we all must be tested. I must have inherited a deficient X chromosome from my father. My own children desperately want to know if they carry the impaired gene from me as some already have children and another is pregnant.

After my daughter tests positive, my grandson is tested and comes back positive, as we suspected. It is a terrible loss to the young couple who have just recently had another child. Testing is delayed for the baby as another loss cannot be levelled at my daughter or her husband at this time.

Without being tested, I now know I have passed this impairment to some of my children and to my grandchild or grandchildren. I watch as my child is crippled with guilt as a carrier, as I am. I know my siblings experience this grief of giving an impairment to their children as well.

The unravelling of emotions occurring in the entire family, including the extended family, is extremely overwhelming. Each day, we hear of another positive test to the impairment for another relative. After months of medical testing, we tally up the total positives. We find that within my line of the family, including my grandmother and father, there are thirteen, both adults and children, affected with the ailment to varying degrees.

The manifestation of the syndrome is unique to everyone affected. Not one person has the exact same symptoms as another. Even the carriers are not just carriers; they have their own exclusive symptoms, ranging from mild to severe, that will be with them for life, increasing in intensity as they become older.

I seek comfort and reassurance from Spirit in my celestial home. Prayers are made for strength, courage, understanding, and acceptance. I reconnect to Saint Anthony each night as I lie down beneath Hana's painting hanging on the wall above my bed. I also reconnect with Hana. It is only going through the testing period that I have thought of her again. We have an answer to her worries and concerns for her children, grandchildren, and now great grandchildren.

I understand Hana so fully now. She did not have any answers but managed to raise her children. Maybe she did not have the impairment herself, and she did not understand them completely while she lived. I feel so much pain for the tragic misunderstandings her girls seemingly suffered at the hands of ignorance from all the professionals they encountered. Hana's next generation of affected children, grandchildren, and great grandchildren have never understood the impairment from a medical perspective. However, they certainly knew the effects from experience.

It is almost too overwhelming to try to comprehend the impact the impairment is making in the last and current generations on this earthly plain. How many are affected by the impairment in the generations since it began is unknown and will never be known. To try to count those with the impairment would be impossible.

Hana is no longer alive on earth, but I feel I still embody her as Asina in the present moment. Having experienced her life and her toils, I feel her confusion about her girls as I feel the same confusion about my generation and my children's and grandchildren's generations. Only now is there acceptance of the syndrome. New research has developed physical, psychological, medical, behavioural, and educational interventions.

We are inundated with professionals in occupational therapy, speech therapy, ophthalmology, behavioural optometry, special education, and other specialists. My daughter and I incorporate them all one by one for my youngest son and for her son. We continue with her daughter, who has since tested positive, although her symptoms are quite different from her brother's.

As a result, every moment of every day is coloured with the latest technique and strategy given to us from the varying disciplines. However, we come to realise the bulk of the work rests on us, the parents, to carry out the specific exercise regime given to us from each professional. We are shown how each exercise is managed, but it is left up to the parents to find time to include the exercises into an already overwhelming day filled with emotional outbursts, language difficulties, eating problems, unbalanced gaits, vision problems, and most of all anxieties with transitions and new environments.

My daughter and I also seek spiritual assistance from the heavenly realm. As mothers we call for help with our children from our spiritual guides, and from my constant heavenly companion Mother Mary. We fear our gentling soul children will most likely not seek careers in the modern world as they get older. They will only experience life through constant care and support on entering the fast-flowing pace of society.

Great mental anguish is felt by both sets of parents, and we seek shelter by moving closer to each other and living with each other's support. My youngest sister and her young child also follow us to a farming region in the countryside that is conducive to the children's needs for a calm environment. Our three families are in constant contact and offer each other and each child much needed support.

By this time, it is obvious that we need a special place to offer physical, psychological, and educational support for the children. My husband and I extend our home by attaching a removal house via a connecting veranda and covered archway. The new house is set up with school rooms, therapy equipment, and an office.

We begin with the assistance of distance education teachers and support workers for the disability. We develop a daily routine of therapy and schoolwork. We set up a school room for each child, so they are not distracted by being together. This is also because they are all different ages, have different physical needs, are at different levels of education. The support worker comes in every other day from the local disability centre to help with physical exercises and reading and writing. We discover our endeavour to teach our children is not as easy as we thought it was going to be. This becomes our learning as well.

We learn about gaze avoidance while trying to get them to make eye contact with us as we teach their lessons. Looking out the window while listening to a story or to instructions becomes the usual position for them. Sitting beside them is also uncomfortable for them as light touches irritate their sensitive skin. Loud noises can startle the gentle souls and cause full-blown emotional outbursts.

We learn that all their sensory inputs are heightened due to the lack of inhibitors in the brain to moderate the resounding stimuli. They can be overwhelmed by sound, emotion, movement, vibration, touch, smell, sight, and taste that ricochet through their bodies until they eventually dissipate and the body returns to equilibrium.

Social interaction is difficult because of their gaze avoidance, limited language skills, unawareness of social norms, heightened arousal amongst crowds of people, and sensitivity to touch. Family gatherings must include acceptance or at least tolerance of unexpected and disruptive behaviour. Managing family interactions is the most difficult as "normal" expectations are not met by some members, including the little ones.

As a counsellor, I have been trained in listening and perceptive skills to try to understand what triggered the unwanted behaviour preceding the outburst. They need professionals who will not expect normal behaviour, such as eye contact, easy transitions, ability to tolerate loud classrooms, sudden noises, severe startled reflexes, and tactile sensitivities.

With an already established career in counselling in relationships, grief, and loss, I now expand my skills and experience counselling families who suffer grief and loss associated with living with and understanding and managing those with disabilities. I return to continue my studies, undertaking a master's degree in counselling in disabilities. For my thesis, I choose to study the impact of genetic disorders on a family to understand behaviours of those with disabilities.

I travel to facilitate workshops and present at conferences for professionals working with families with neurogenetic disabilities. I concentrate on presenting workshops on educating children with these disabilities through my experience of teaching my own children of two generations. I present strategies and methods of teaching children with environmental sensitivities, anxiety, and intellectual impairment associated with neurogenetic disorders to assist teachers who encounter our children. I tell and re-tell my own experiences of my family members who present with the disorder.

Together with my daughter and sister, I establish an incorporated association in our state to contact others with the genetic disorder. The association blossoms into a vehicle for forming friendships with other families suffering from a disorder. It also encourages me to incorporate relationship counselling for couples who are experiencing a partner or children with the impairment. I also concentrate on techniques and strategies to teach these gentle souls and support and assist the parent who has passed the gene onto his or her child. I also counsel the parent who becomes the companion to the gentle soul and needs extra support to understand and manage family members with the impairment.

For five or six years, we undertake full-time care and support for our own children with the impairment, for those without the impairment, and for each member of our families. We attend regular appointments with professional therapists and undertake daily exercise routines with new strategies with our children who have the disability. We organise meetings of the group in the newly attached office and meeting rooms, and travel to incorporate other regions of our state. We design workshops, we organise conferences, and counsel many families.

The rigid regime begins to exhaust us as we carriers also suffer effects of the disorder. As the children continue to grow, we learn that we need to introduce them to society with support workers to assist us and help them interact with others. Ways to do this include special education classes at school, outings to swimming pools, sporting activities, or entertainment such as going to cinemas, shopping centres, or concerts.

Every event undertaken saps our energy, patience, and time further. When our energy is completely spent, we close the association and help our members incorporate into a national corporation. Having experienced the world of disabilities, we now have the courage to continue for our children and take them into adulthood. I continue to counsel families dealing with disabilities.

As each new companion soul in the family emerges from infancy, he or she is naturally introduced to the gentle souls in the family. The companion children and the gentle souls know there is no difference, they are one, and each has his or her place.

Chapter 11

MARY DALE

Family issues have taken their toll in each of our families during the time we have spent with the group. We need to attend to cracked relationships we have neglected since being immersed in the world of disabilities. We have catch-up work to do with the companion souls who have weathered the storm of disabilities with us.

My youngest daughter without the impairment begins to show chronic signs of an illness. I am drawn away from my career in disabilities and I convert to part-time counselling in the home office to be able to tend to her needs with her children.

Life becomes hectic for me bouncing from one family member to another and from one specific need to another. I need all the strength I can absorb from my heavenly companions. They come to me in the form of visits, unexpected messages, and powerful interactions during my nightly travels to the heavenly realm.

I call to Mother Mary as I waft between sleep and awake. "You are a mother, and you know the pain of your child. I will do anything for my children as you showed us how to do. Please show me that you are with me to address the needs of my children. I know you understand what I need more than I do. I trust you and your son

Jesus will attend to the needs of my children. I trust you completely to hear and answer and support me."

My answer comes weeks or months later in a vision when I am travelling in the heavenly realm. In this travel time, I am looking for my one-year-old grandchild, a companion soul, who is missing. I search the office building on all levels where my unwell daughter, his mother, has her business, and I can't find him. I can't find his parents either. I need to find her child. I know I must look for him and look after him as they are also missing.

I get to the ground level, walk outside to the busy city street, and search for him there. I finally find him under a bus seat at the edge of the road. I gasp in horror as I realise that if he moves, he will roll onto the road and be hit by a passing car. Holding my breath in fear, I lunge and grab him just before he stumbles onto the road. I pick him up and hug him to myself. In my mind, I try to figure out what to do. *I must get him to their home. If I catch a bus to the inner city, I can change buses and get the bus to his home.*

I hear inside me that I need to catch the bus that has just pulled into the stop in front of me. With great doubt if this is the right bus, I get on this bus, sit down, and hold tight to my grandchild. We travel through the busy city, past the outer city suburbs, and merge out onto the highway. I don't know where we are heading, but I need to trust we are going in the right direction as I don't recognise this area.

We travel for over an hour and the child has fallen asleep in my lap. I notice we are coming into a small country town and the bus is stopping at a shopping centre. It is the end of the line, and we all need to exit. I pick up my sleeping grandchild and get off the bus. I try to figure out where I am and where to go to next. I am panicked and afraid.

I walk into the shopping centre and buy some food for us. I wander around looking for other buses that might be going wherever

I am supposed to be heading. I am completely lost. I start walking around the outside of the centre, carrying a sleeping baby over my shoulder, looking for clues as to what I am to do next.

Then I hear an inner message: "Catch the next bus to Mary Dale."

I don't know where Mary Dale is. I have never heard of it, but I search the terminal for the bus to Mary Dale. I find it in the last parking bay, and I am the only one who gets on the bus. I hold my child tight and watch as we travel onto a country road towards a country town. After about another hour, we reach the town. I recognise the town as I often pass through it to get to my home in the country. I start to feel relief as I am starting to understand that I am taking my child home with me to the country valley of lush farms.

I wake from my sleep. It is morning, and I am in my own bed with the sun shining through the parted curtains. I lie with my rosary beads in my hand knowing that my plea for help and support has been answered. All I must do now is wait until the message manifests in real time. For now, though, I know I must name my valley farm Mary Dale. I think to myself, *That's strange. We do live in a valley.* I have no idea what the visit to the heavenly home means. I guess I must follow the daily messages that will lead me onto the right bus to get me where I am to go.

My thoughts take me to a recent encounter we had with an aerial photographer who was passing through our country region a while back. He was taking photos of individual farms and selling his photos to the families. We took the opportunity to have our property captured by photograph and we have it hanging in our kitchen. Now I have a photo of Mary Dale. I immediately assume that I am in the right place to encounter what is going to happen next in the life of our Mary Dale family.

With the gradual realisation that the disability is not going to leave us we must endeavour to bring the family back together after the tsunami. We must learn how to meld both sides of the family, to bring our gentle souls together with our companion souls. Both the tsunami and the disability must not take the prominent position in the family.

Daily life now includes training the gentle souls to accept another change in the family. The support for the next trauma is undertaken with great love and allowance for all. After a bitter separation, my daughter Nettie is coming home with her children, the youngest just turning three.

Nettie arrives late one night after another marital confrontation. She starts setting up Mary Dale as a home where she will live with her children until she recovers. Nettie teaches her children, "No one gets left behind."

Mary Dale has now become a focal point of change as office furniture and belongings are moved to make room for a new family to integrate into her area. We assist as Nettie prepares the children to start at the little local school just three minutes' drive from the farm. The school is tucked in beside the flowing creek right in the middle of the tiny farming community. It becomes the children's introduction to country living. This move for them is the manifestation of their coming home to themselves. The great spiritual designer is moving us all onwards.

With only twenty children in the school, the children are given close personal attention, which balances them with the trauma they are living through. They catch the little school bus to and from school and are dropped off at the front entrance to our home. The sports oval is two kilometres away and we gather to watch each sport's day with the local farmers and their children.

Nettie and the children live with us for over a year. As she recovers, she finds a job, returns to her studies part time, and purchases a home for her and the children only thirty minutes from Mary Dale.

The children settle well and start new schools. Life eases for them until she is diagnosed two years later with early-stage cervical cancer, for which she seeks medical treatment. Life tries to surge forward after her operation, but within another two years the cancer has returned, and she seeks further treatment. Only a matter of months later, the cancer returns and becomes terminal.

Mary Dale slowly transforms again as there becomes a need to again incorporate them into our family life at Mary Dale. We can't face fatal concepts fully while we are living with her again, but innately, we know what could happen.

We design a new kitchen for Mary Dale with Nettie's creative input. She becomes involved wholeheartedly. We make sure that the extension is huge enough to fit the whole family when we gather. We make allowances in the size of the room for both dining tables and sets of chairs. There is seating capacity for twenty people in the dining area. We also add an additional length to make an area large enough to accommodate a family sitting room with adequate lounge chairs.

The builders come in every day and Nettie and I watch their progress together. The activity keeps us focused on life. Palliative support nurses also arrive every day. It becomes obvious that Nettie is building a home for her children so that she can feel easier knowing where they will be living when she leaves without them. The building project keeps her alert to the outside world through her pain and her slow demise.

Building continues and bedrooms are decorated in the colours the children choose. A new bedroom is designed downstairs in the unit for Nettie to have her own privacy. I tend to the children upstairs in the redecorated area of bedrooms, bathroom, and sitting area. The kitchen will become a separate community area connected to the house by a veranda. This is where we will all meet.

The nightly prayer meetings cement the wonder of and reliance on Mother Mary, Jesus, and all his angels into all the souls in Mary Dale. It isn't just a farm or a property anymore. It is a haven, a sanctuary, a blessed dwelling for the broken, the disabled, the mother, the children, the old, and the beloved daughter who will never spirituality leave this place. Every night, we take turns choosing a personal intention and write it in the journals we are creating. Our intentions for the present moments give us the strength to get through each day.

I can see the gatherings of nightly rosaries after all chores are complete for the day may not give us the miracle we are praying for, that of saving our beloved's life. Our earnest prayers rise to heaven while we sit with our beloved as the central focus amongst giggles, candles, joviality, intentions, seriousness, muted light, tears, and personal prayers. We pray for the miracle that we will need to save us from complete and utter despair and annihilation if she leaves us.

Nettie doesn't see the opening of the kitchen as she must leave before it is finished. All our lives take a sharp turn towards living without her. Mary Dale's community kitchen and home begins without her physical presence, but her spiritual presence remains constantly.

We all must create a new normal, and we learn what that means day by day as each issue arises. We are all barely managing to complete our daily chores before bedtime, and the exhaustion of grief overcomes all of us. We cannot continue the gatherings of prayers without feeling overwhelmed and unable to focus anymore. Meetings now occur at the end of my bed, where grieving is allowed.

Every moment is spent securing trust and boundaries for the young family who are trying to process the loss of their mother and integrating within the world of disabilities and advancing age. No one is sure how to go about this constant process, but because there is love and belonging in all occupants of the household, everything eventually comes around to work in all our favours.

Chapter 12

PERSPECTIVE

It is difficult for our gentle ones to process the loss of their loved one even though we talk to her, for she is still with us. Nettie said to me, "This is too much for this family," as she witnessed the strain on all the souls within the family. She was referring, of course, to her own children, then to myself as her gentle soul mother, and to her sisters as gentle souls. She also knew it was too much for her gentle soul brother and our two gentle soul grandchildren. It was, of course, too much for the other significant companion soul members of the family.

We know now that the miracle we were praying for all those nights in prayer gatherings with Nettie were for the after-years. Then, we build further trust and honesty between all of us, and we all find a steadier footing in undertaking the process of grieving together in our own ways. With sensitivities at their height within every member of the family, the mammoth task of keeping our mental health secure becomes our permanent duty.

No sooner has the grieving become the focus, COVID hits across the world and drives us all in different directions. I can see now that my health was already declining long before I stepped out of the family business because of the COVID restrictions on my health and because of being an elder.

I know now I will not be going back into the business as I once was. I will continue the bookwork and staffing issues by working at home. It is not just because of COVID; it is time to retire from the manual work and keep my own consultant work going at half pace. Already I have taken many falls at work that twice resulted in a broken wrist. Handling of product and standing on my feet all day had to cease because of excruciating pain in my back.

I spend the days during the next two years coping with heart issues that were connected to my back pain. I am learning what I can now do and what I can no longer do. During these early days, I can barely walk the high steps up from my home office to the kitchen and my living quarters upstairs. To compensate for this, each day I walk the back ramp to the car, drive down the hill to my front office downstairs, and drive back again. I sleep, eat, and make sure that I walk a small amount each day.

I can no longer stand in the kitchen preparing and cooking large family meals and clashing with young adults each day. Gathering in shopping malls is also not inviting to me anymore after falling and injuring myself a few times trying to get the grocery trolley down the incline in the supermarket carpark. I have found online shopping a great asset given that the COVID infections are also rife amongst crowds.

The trauma has taken its toll on an aging gentle soul's body, and it seems that my outer edge has been worn down. Any physical and emotional pressure now scratches me like an abrasive cleaner on glass. It is time to recoil into my spiritual life inside my inner sanctuary and accept who I am.

The younger ones are considerate with my waning body and are adjusting accordingly. They are accustomed to me hitting the ground running each morning as I spring out of bed to prepare lunches, drop the children off at school, and then go off to work. In the afternoon is a rush to buy meals for the day, prepare them, do laundry, shower, and then invite nightly family grieving gatherings at the foot of my bed.

COVID continues to separate us, as the family of grown children begin living independently downstairs in Nettie's unit and using the small kitchen she used when she lived on her own downstairs. The younger ones take great care not to intermingle with us, their elders, or with those with the disabilities.

On good weather days, we meet outside in the open shelter for outdoor living and wear masks when we meet. When other family members visit us in the same way, we each bring our own food. We gather for birthdays and other special days, and we interact with each other in a newfound way to enjoy each other's company.

The pressure of being the one who organises everything has changed. Instead of buying food for all, cooking all the family meals, and serving and cleaning, independence has begun and has released me from enormous tasks.

It is wonderful to watch as the young adults make their ways in life and return the love given to them by the adults in the family during the long journey through grief and sadness. They are building new lives that their mother would be proud of. They are entering the world as independently as possible as they undertake their higher education levels.

Mary Dale is no longer dishevelled as it was during the survival phase and running the businesses seven days a week. Since the COVID restrictions, my husband Sentel and I have never had so much time at home. The house, gardens, and lawns are his top priorities, as Mary Dale is coming alive again slowly. My extra time now allows me to sit in my sanctuary and mediate, pray, write, and listen to my ancestors talk to me.

Today, I think it is Paddy who makes an appearance in my travelling moments in half-sleep. He comes with another visitor who I recognise as a nephew. He has found me to tell me how he is struggling to come to terms with the loss of his brother. I know my nephew is still alive, so I reach out and hug him and offer my healing love. He hugs me back and tells me, "My brother has died." Indeed, his brother has died, and I realise he is struggling in life without his brother. I hug him and pray for healing for him.

In the same image sits a man on the sidelines, who silently lets me know of the name of Paddy. He is an elderly man, with beautifully kept short grey hair and wearing a nice suit. He is very gentle and kind.

I stir awake and I'm left worrying for my nephew. I think to myself, *I must contact him.*

For a few days, I am left thinking it must be Paddy who is trying to tell me something. I know he is familiar. Is this Clarrie's brother who is visiting me? I think about him, and I think it could be him from my visits as Hana, although he is older now.

I contact my paternal cousin and seek information. She sends a photo of Paddy, but it is not him. Then I tell her, "I think it must be Clarrie then. Do you have a photo of Clarrie?"

She sends a photo of Clarrie when he was older. "Yes," I tell her, "That's Clarrie."

She tells me, "I was told that he was a soft, gentle man who loved to play his own musical instruments. He was also very sensitive, and suffered ill health, and Hana became his caregiver."

In the vision, Clarrie says nothing to me but acknowledges me with a smile. Is he telling me that his brother has died too? From my searches, I see that they died only weeks apart. Paddy died first. Indeed, his brother had died. Clarrie died only weeks later. Is this him grieving for his lost brother? Why has he come to me? Is this just information he is telling me so I will recognise him?

I have recognised him. He just looks at me as I look back at him. He is sitting on a bench seat outside our old beachside business. I also know through my family that this is the same place where both

Paddy and Clarrie arrived from Ireland over 100 years ago by ship and landed at the wharf of this seaside town. The two boys arrived here on their own, knowing no one and having to survive on their own without their mother or father. I now remember Hana and her family also arrived at this same wharf years earlier than the brothers.

Of course, he would come to this beach town where he began his life so many years ago. I am surprised that I too came to this beachside town to live with my family years ago.

Many people through the last century have sat on this bench seat to watch the ships arrive at the end of the long pier that leads out to the deep water for mooring and unloading passengers and cargo. From the seat, you can see the path going down the hill to the shoreline below and the pier stretching out from the beach towards the horizon. This is the place where Clarrie and Hana spent many happy holidays with their family.

So many times, I sat on the seat with my children as they were growing up. So many times, I walked with them along the pier, not knowing that my family arrived here many years ago. As a child myself, I climbed on the cargo ships that only moored there in later years.

The strange thing is that days after this awakening, before I found out any information from my cousin, I sought Spirit for something to let me know I was on the right track thinking it was Clarrie who could have introduced an impairment into the family long ago.

Now I see Clarrie sitting on the seat reminiscing as he watches himself arrive. He is meeting me here as I wait for him years later to acknowledge his role in the impairment in the family. What an acknowledgment of my family and my beginnings. What love of a gentle soul. I feel so blessed that he has come to me to encourage me to keep telling our story together.

I no longer doubt that an impairment can begin with poverty and lack of nutrition, use of alcohol and other substances, lack of health, and many stresses on the mind, body, and soul. The DNA can change and can cause genetic anomalies that can be inherited for generations to come.

Poor little Anne, their mother, was left so malnourished by her mother Mary. After suffering poverty and sickness, Mary died so young and left her child to cope with a weakened body. Anne perhaps was the one who inherited the beginning of her mother's unstable X chromosome in her DNA.

When Anne birthed Clarrie, it appears that she gave him the unstable X chromosome inherited from her mother. He gave his unstable X chromosome, inherited from his mother and his grandmother to all his daughters. I have inherited Clarrie's unstable X chromosome and I too have passed it on to my children.

In my children's generation, and their children's generation of gentle souls, they have chosen not to have more children, but to live happily with their gentle souls and to watch as the impairment ends.

Our family of gentle souls has endured through nearly two hundred years of transformation in the world. They have encountered horrific wars, the slaughter of many, and devastation of the face of the earth, including climate change, pollution of our oceans, our lands, and our minds, and nuclear war. The world at large is now reacting to the misuse of its wonders and its powers.

No longer do we have the natural masters of the earth who tended to her needs by taking only what they needed. Now we have greed so great the earth itself is buckling under the pressure of being scavenged for its minerals. Her waterways are polluted with the excess rubbish we take from her lands, and her lands are filled with chemicals to grow the food we eat.

There are amongst us the gentle souls who have come just to be the love and gentleness the people of the world need in this transforming time on the earth. This transformation is now essential to the earth's existence. If we become extinct on this earth, we have not listened to the gentle souls who have only come to make sure we are gently brought back to our souls in this time of reformation.

Our souls know the truth that we live in today. We must return to our consciousnesses that exist eternally, from generation to generation, emitting the message to come back to our souls. Our souls know how to love the earth, to love its creatures, and to love its people. Listen, if you hear the call of your soul.

Chapter 13

GENTLING SOULS

As I reach out to Clarrie from my earthly realm, Clarrie reaches out to me from his heavenly realm. He is entering my life on earth, and we are beginning to communicate together about how being a gentling soul really feels for each of us. I feel today how it would have felt for him long ago, and he feels how it is for me today. The two realms are melding as we acknowledge each other's existence in this same moment.

Of course, it was hard for him with his sensitivities to his body and emotions. Of course, it is hard for me. It takes twice as long for me, and it would have been for him as well, to come out of overwhelming circumstances as one would without the anomaly on the DNA. Emotions for gentling souls are hard to keep under control, if excessive reactions are not taken care of.

All the skills I have accumulated as a counsellor I use with myself. I understand Clarrie would not have had these skills, and excessive drinking is one method which is still used today for less severely affected gentling souls. His daughters would have had mild to moderate symptoms, not severe symptoms as in the next generation.

Still, his girls would have had symptoms of high anxiety and sensitivity to all their senses of sight, sound, taste, touch, hearing, movement, and emotions. They may have had other physical symptoms such as nervousness, heart murmurs, low muscle tone, eye problems, and awkward gait, to name a few.

Neither he nor Hana would have understood the complexity of the physical and emotional ailments their girls displayed. They only had to handle each one as it presented. I am ever grateful for the study that allows me to serve my own children and others who suffer from great anguish with damage to their DNA.

Teaching my gentle children with more severe symptoms how to cope with their emotions is imperative. I remember watching my child sitting on the bed trying to take control of his emotions, by rocking back and forth saying over and over, "I can do this. I can do this!" I watched in amazement at his persistence in learning to soothe himself.

I must say that it certainly looks humorous to others when you wrap your child in a blanket like a sausage to calm the movement sensitivity still being experienced from a car, plane, boat or train ride, or any other strong movement. I do the same for myself after a long, hard day of stress, movement, and emotions. For anyone else, the feeling is like having to experience your sea legs after being on the ocean for days.

Excessive experiences for these severely affected children/adults can result in overreactions. They can act out unexpectedly by hitting you, running out onto the road, running away, climbing a tree, throwing objects, sitting down in the middle of a thoroughfare, or other impulsive behaviours.

Counselling parents and family members is crucial to their understanding that their child/adult is in a hyperaroused state. The person needs understanding and special treatment to help him or her come out of this unintentional behaviour. From the outside, it looks like the situation needs to be manhandled, but that is the worst thing to do. Touching someone in this state can heighten their sensitivities, which will only cause more stimuli to their bodies and to their hyperactivity.

Having been in many of these occurrences with my own children and with clients, it is best to sit quietly away from the child/adult in an outburst and speak in a soft, quiet, non-threatening voice. Describe the trigger that sent him or her into an overstimulated state. For example, the person may have been frightened when the alarm went off unexpectedly, or someone said something he or she didn't like or understand, or the person was told to finish and move on before he or she was ready.

So many things can set off an outburst. Sometimes you do not know what it is and the person doesn't know what it is. You must find the trigger by guessing until the person lets you know by his or her reaction which it is. Once you find out what caused the outburst, then it is possible to enact out the calming techniques with the person. As parents or workers, you must become astute enough with the person to watch for triggers and be able to help the person understand his or her own behaviour.

Describing the behaviour for the person will give the person an understanding of himself or herself and the feeling of being heard. Then you will be able to teach the person calming techniques to ease himself or herself in the situation. Life can become hectic for you as the parent or the caregiver, as it is difficult not to become tense and aroused to the person's level of distress.

Of course, you are of no help to the person if you panic, become angry, and yell at him or her to calm down, or even hit back or pick up any object you can throw. He or she has just triggered you and the situation is no longer viable to a calm outcome. This is where many families, workers, and school staff are taken to defend themselves. Then there is an unavoidable confrontation with a third party, like police or social workers. Many gentling souls find themselves in protective care and institutions for the mentally challenged, and they should not be there.

Understanding gentling souls and the role they play in our society today takes great fortitude for their families and support workers. No one has the answers for all the questions, but to see them distressed and unable to function in the environment they live in becomes a social concern.

Living in a calm environment is essential for both parents, especially for the one who has the anomaly on his or her DNA. This is also important for the child/adult and for other members of the family.

However, living in this environment for the companion souls is not easy. It takes great understanding and patience to learn that gentling souls' reactions are not personal to them. They are just trying to fit into a world that does not allow for what looks like socially unacceptable behaviour. They will tell you what is acceptable to them through acting out behaviours, unless you can teach them to speak what they want to tell you.

Try to help them find the words, which is difficult for those who are verbally challenged. It takes great patience from any companion soul not to aggravate the gentling soul by expecting his or her own "normal" behaviour from that person.

Mind you, all gentling souls will try with all their might to fit into the family, into conversations, family activities, school activities, and social activities. Exceptions must be made continually, and impatience of others can trigger uncomfortable outcomes for the gentling souls and the rest of the family or group.

Life entails working around normal activities and making them also suitable for the gentling souls. Time constraints, weather conditions, storm clouds, loud environments, and crowded malls are only a fraction of the occurrences that need to be accounted for.

A parent's life becomes dictated by the constraints of the gentling souls in the family, perhaps in lieu of a partner's wishes, a family's wishes, a school's wishes, and of normality in general. "Normal" then involves incorporating a gentling soul's needs into your life. Not many can do this, and many families split up from the pressure on their emotional levels.

I spent many years facilitating workshops for professionals, parents, and families. Counselling many gentling souls, and their support workers, parents and families became my career for many years until I had to return to my family who needed my support.

At this point in my life, I began to realise that the Divine too had a role to play in the gentling souls' lives. He created them for a reason, for when they are living in a placid environment, they are naturally gentle and loving and would not harm anyone. They teach those who open their souls to hear that they gather souls together. All they desire is for the family to be together where they feel loved and safe and can love in return.

It takes great patience, understanding, compassion, kindness, and care to assist gentling souls who are uncomfortable in "normal" surrounds and who, like all humans, long for someone to understand and love them. We all are truly like them, for that is all we really want in life: to be understood and loved and to love in return.

They show us how to dispel the myths of wanting more than we can manage, of seeking more than we can have, and of asking for more than we need. Their wants are simple, their needs are basic, their love is pure, and their giving is Divine.

I have taught all my children that the Divine is why we are here. The gentling souls can understand and believe in the Divine who created the trees, flowers, animals, stars, sun, and moon. They know from an early age how to rely on others for their safety and security. We see them as dependent on us but we are dependent on them to be able to see life through their eyes and through our own souls. They are pure love. They are not malicious, but they can manipulate to have their own needs met. At times, they must manipulate because we do not give them our understanding to help them meet their needs.

They are not their bodies; they are their souls. They remain their souls while on earth. They are here to teach us how to become our souls as well, to see life through their gentleness, dependence on, and love for others. They teach us that the Divine has placed gentling souls into our lives for us to know that the Divine is ever present in our lives through them.

All gentle souls are stirring on earth now, as the gathering of souls of ancient times is stirring and we are forming together with them again, bringing the intention of long ago into fruition. The ancient ones have been waiting for me to arrive in this place in time. They have been waiting for me to reach back to them, to understand them, to seek each one of them out, to accept them, to love them, and to free them of the ages of denial they have endured and of the isolation on earth of their gentle souls.

We are to heal each other. As we heal each other, we heal our places in heaven and our places on earth. We heal for all time all our gentling souls, and all those who have been touched by gentling souls in space and time. This is the existence of the gentling souls who have passed by to get to this present moment.

We are here now to become open and heal with the past gentle souls, to listen to and to believe in the mission of being the gentling souls who have come to the earth with love and understanding for this present moment. We have each had our own role to play in this great mystery of life that is still existing in the past, the present, and the future.

The time is now. The world needs the goodness of the gentling souls to change the old thinking of "kill or be killed" or "an eye for an eye," of one dominant species over other species, of one race over another, and of one gender over another.

In an attempt, to offer humanity a replacement to the continued use of violence, hatred, revenge, and war, the gentling souls bring divine gentleness, love, acceptance, and compassion to our world. These souls, described by many as imperfect humans, have come with divine love to save the earth from the ravages of human ignorance, chemical warfare, nuclear weapons, and extinction.

Chapter 14

REUNION

This is the moment in time that the gentling souls in our family have all been waiting for: the meeting of the first gentling souls with the last of the gentling souls here on earth and in heaven.

Anne and her son Clarrie are the first gentling souls in our family. I, Asina, and my last gentling soul grandchild, are the ending. We are together at last; we are the beginning and the end in our gentle soul family. Great celebration begins to encompass all our gentle and companion souls, the past with the present.

It is overwhelming to realise that I am witnessing and experiencing the long line of ancestors coming together to celebrate the culmination of gentle lives already lived on earth mingling with my family of gentling souls still here on earth. A great transformation on earth and in heaven is occurring in this troubled world.

As I walk outside today, I look at each flower I pass, each tree, each bird, insect, and butterfly. I believe each is in its right place to amass with all of God's creation. We are within the Divine as heaven and earth come together in these days of great triumph.

Even though wars rage, violence against each other continues, and earth is crying for restoration, gentling souls and companions are listening to the murmuring of peace at all costs growing into a mighty roar. There is a rising happening in unison with the call for peace and love to reign among all the many gentling souls and companion souls. In our own unique roles, we are bringing healing to a world that is ready for the change. It is happening now.

Rivers are flowing cleaner, oceans are being cleaned, the land is being renewed, the climate is being remedied, the earth is calling for nourishment. We are no longer individually racing through life in a whirlwind of panic and frustration to obtain all we desire. We are walking peacefully through life in a heavenly formation of gentling souls with our companion souls, designing peace wherever we are present.

Look around and you will see the great formation of souls who are flying together amongst us. Through all the images in our media that show the devastation of the earth, there amongst the rubble lie the hearts and souls of the many gentling souls and their companions throughout the world.

You may scroll through your media to see what is happening, but you need to turn it off for a while and walk outside. See the beauty of nature. Watch those who are planting their own needs. Watch parents schooling their own children. Accept those who wish to work from home amongst their families. Love those who protect the gentle ones and the aged and sick from COVID infections. Bow to those who have saved many lives and put their own lives on the line to do so.

What have we accomplished in the isolation but the need to be together with our loved ones in forgiveness and acceptance? Healing of the planet has begun. We will rebuild everything that hatred, war, killing, and revenge has taken from us. To only have the thoughts and intentions of love and renewal of the earth is all we need to overcome the almighty forces of hatred, anger, and murder.

Each day, the remembrance of our ancestors, their struggles, fears, and love, keep us alive. We are able to live another day to carry on their needs for love and acceptance of their mission. My family is the last generation in our family of gentling souls, the ones who came to bring love to the broken world, with their imperfect bodies, who put to shame those who look upon them and see only imperfections.

Their imperfections are in their bodies, as they see it, but their souls are perfect and made in the image of the Divine. The Divine has used them to bring his peace and love to the world. There is only honour and love for all the gentling souls and their companions who dared to enter the world—a world seeking perfection that will never be found here. Perfection is love—Divine love—and the Divine is melded in the souls of the gentling souls and their companions. Divine love dwells in all souls. Listen as the Divine calls you home to yourself—home to your soul.

As the urge to step out of the shadow of insignificance roars alive in me, I see now that I have been, as my ancestors were, eager to step out into the world. I have been nervous not to ignite my anxieties, but willing to bolster my energy to such a level that I can meet any tribulation life can give me. I know I can do this to myself. As I grow older, I seem to be losing energy to maintain the level of resistance needed to maintain life in the "normal" range.

I have an abundance of willpower to challenge myself to reach the level needed to overcome adversity of working in the "normal" range. However, I question more often now, as a gentling soul, if I should continue to maintain "normal" when I am a gentling soul. Have I struggled long enough trying to be what I am not? Is this the letting go of expected behaviour? Have I tried with all my might to be what others expect of me? What have I expected from myself? Who am I? I am a gentling soul.

I need a quiet environment. I need to recoil. I need to hibernate. I need to feel as I do. I need to write as I do. I need to be my soul. I become cranky now when I am expected to be as others want me to be. I am cranky with myself when I expect myself to be as I expect me to be, and I can't make it to my own expectations. I blame myself or I blame others for my inadequacies. I have been doing it for so long. I have hated myself that I can't keep up for so long, that I am not understood, that I give myself such a hard time of it. I alone give myself a hard time because I can't keep up. However, I am, and have always been, a gentling soul.

This search for my ancestors and finding the beginning of the gentling souls in the family has been for me a journey to find myself, to accept myself, and to honour myself. There is no one so cruel as I am to myself. I have accustomed myself to the mores of the day. Since my birth, I have tried to become what I was never destined to become: "normal." I am, and have always been, a gentling soul.

At the conclave of souls long before this lifetime, I answered the call to become a gentling soul for the good of other generations within my family of souls. I recognise myself as living other lifetimes, waiting to become a gentling soul. As the time came for me to present on earth as a gentling soul, I agreed to live a lifetime of being a gentling soul. It has not been easy. I have been ridiculed, mocked, manipulated, abused, and abandoned for my sensitivities, my nervousness, my anxieties, and especially for choosing to live in my soul for this lifetime.

My inadequacies have been a trial for me to manage, as they took me far from self-care and self-acceptance. I did not understand the anomaly that I came to earth with and I lived with it most of my life. I misunderstood myself for so long that it became a discrepancy in me rather than a blessing that I behold with honour now.

Looking with deep understanding and compassion towards my ancestors, I reach out to them in love to heal myself and them. They too did not understand what they were carrying as part of their physical makeup. I'm sure that vexed them with self-doubt and self-judgment, as I suffered for too long not knowing who I was.

As each moment passes in each day, I encounter the wonderful world of spirit. I unravel the mystical adventure of knowing and releasing the pain of the history of misunderstanding. I see and feel the passing of time as another opening on the path to self-approval.

Recently, in talking with my daughter, who also lived for years not understanding her complexities, I was able to tell her of my enlightenment. In this conversation, with three generations of gentling souls present, I attempted to compare our individual experiences. "I became aware of my impairment when I had passed middle age. I had spent most of my life trying to be what I thought I needed to be, but I continually struggled with my physically sensitivities. I thought I was to blame for my inadequacies, and my self-image and self-judgment was severely misconstrued."

My daughter acknowledged the complexities I had lived with as I continued in recognising her physical struggle until her early adult years. "I know this of you Mum."

"Yes, and you my darling, struggled with your self-image all through your young years into adulthood, until you became aware of your own differences in your body."

"Yes, I know I did Mum." Once again, she accepted what I was saying with sad recognition of her early life.

Then I spoke to her young adult daughter. "You, my beautiful one, you tested positive as a baby, and you have known all your life of your differences. You have navigated your life brilliantly by accepting that it was only a physical anomaly, and it did not define you. You did not blame yourself for your sensitivities."

My granddaughter smiled. "Yes Grandma, I know." She could see herself in comparison to her mother and her grandmother.

Lastly, I spoke to them of our past generational gentling souls who knew nothing of what science has found since their lives here on earth. "What an insight they would have experienced had they known the reason for their own discrepancies during their lifetimes. They are aware now. We can only feel tremendous pain for their misunderstandings of themselves and the misconceptions of their loved ones and others in society. As we are becoming aware of the complexities of being gentling souls, I believe we heal through understanding ourselves more, and we can heal our past generations of gentling souls."

We all bowed our heads in silence with the enormity of the truth and thanked God for our understanding.

During the day, I sat with my husband, told him of the findings, and my acceptances of my day. In doing so, I was able for the first time to tell him, "I am so not like you. You have your own peculiarities and I have mine. I have lived believing that I could not keep up with you, that I suffered physical complications that could never be explained or connected to the anomaly I live with.

"Now I understand that my belief system was misconstrued for many years. I thought I had done something to bring about my own lack of physical abilities. As I grow older, these physical abilities are becoming physical disabilities. They are on a continuum to regenerate with each new cell division that I experience in my body each day."

There was complete silence from him as he tried to digest what was happening to me in the present moment. My inability to keep pace with him physically, even though I am younger, is a result of the variance in my DNA reacting within an aging body and a stressful life.

"Well," he said after some thought, "we will just have to adjust the pace and the commitments we undertake and prepare for a life from here on in for a gentle soul. I think I may have overestimated your physical ability all these years to keep up with me in physically running the property and the two businesses as you always have."

I nod my head as I walk off to make us a cup of tea, then to come sit beside him as we watch our favourite television show together.

Chapter 15

CELEBRATIONS

I wake this morning on the first day of December, with the first of the summer rains gently falling on the lush growth of my plants all around me. The light rain on the roses that are radiating their second blooms becomes like diamond droplets gathering on their petals. The roses are speaking their language of beauty and peace so eloquently while adorning my garden and spreading their perfume through the moist air.

I feel exhilarated as Christmas is nearly here. Summer is promising to be hot, yet today it is cool for this time of the year. Family members are preparing to attend our gathering for Christmas for the first time in years.

While I flit through my memories of Christmases past, I come to the more recent Christmas I remember so vividly: Hana's first Christmas in her new country, the one that I very much enjoyed being a part of.

I reminisce as I sit watching the rain ease. *What a different Christmas that was for me, one with a distinct, traditional Irish flavour mixed with a truly Australian hot summer Christmas Day. We were still so new to this country. I relished the feeling of the newness for my country's Christmas style of sunshine and heat with homemade water slides and trough dipping for keeping the children cool.*

I so loved the hot midday dinner Ma baked in the old combustion oven that heated the whole house. The smell of the plum puddings soaked in rum and packed with mixed dried fruit as well as the iced Christmas cake with thick marzipan icing were special treats for all of us.

The amazing thing for all of us young ones that year was that Father Christmas made it all the way to the southern hemisphere. He brought gifts to all of us. He left each gift under the large spindly pine tree that Pa had cut down, put in a large open drum from the barn, and helped decorate.

On my return from this Christmas, I awoke to my own Christmas Day about to begin with my own family. At that time, I came home with the knowledge and experience of how Christmas started many generations ago with our first Irish/Australian family. From this visit, I truly became one with my ancestors through their joy of celebrations. This Christmas was also our first significant celebration in our new home.

This old Irish/Australian tradition of coming together and celebrating Christmas has been handed down to Hana's children, grandchildren, great grandchildren, and onwards. From their first Christmas, I was able to see how my family has evolved into "true blue Aussies." However, our past became indelibly imprinted into my soul at that Christmas and I wanted to bring their joy with me into the next generation.

In the early days, they did eventually learn to climatise to their new country with big, hot dinners becoming a thing of the past with the Australian heat. In this generation, what we now call a truly Australian Christmas is when the family is celebrating together at the beach, in the cities, or in the country with a barbeque, a leg of ham, and fresh seafood.

When presents are unwrapped, food is eaten, and kids are riding around on new bicycles or frolicking in the swimming pool, then young and old alike settle in for a nap until the cool of the afternoon. Then we will meet again on the beach, in a park, or in the paddock for the Christmas family cricket match. This is a very serious match with great competition among the family members.

After meeting my ancestors, Christmas has become for me not so much about the food, the presents, and the game of cricket. It is all that, but it is also an end of a season in life and a new beginning of a new life approaching. This year, I have a need to recreate their passion and enthusiasm for beginning again by developing a new tradition that encompasses the old traditions they brought with them from Ireland.

We will follow our Aussie traditions. However, this Christmas is the culmination of years of grief and mourning the inability to have life as expected. I am embracing life as a gentling soul who sees life through the eyes of love and simplicity of the gentle souls. Gentle souls love the joy of giving and receiving, and they love the feast and cricket game. They also love the intimacy of being together with loved ones.

The gentle souls' Christmas emotions start as soon as retailers put their Christmas decorations up in their stores. The excitement and anticipation begins inside their bodies. The build-up affects the gentle soul adults in the same way children anticipate Christmas.

They become overloaded emotionally and physically, and by the end of Christmas Day, there is a release of excitement. After Christmas, it takes twice as long for a gentling soul to find his or her physical and emotional equilibrium as it does anyone else.

That has become the rule of thumb we use for the gentling souls in the family. We know that it will take twice as long for a gentling soul to process his or her excitement, fear, loss, anger, or any other emotion than a "normal" reaction takes for anyone else.

I remember a Christmas time when I was a small, gentle soul child at my paternal grandmothers. All of her twenty grandchildren met together at her home near the beach. She emulated her mother Hana by creating Christmas as a celebration of family with beautiful, home-cooked hot food and many presents under the tree. As children, we did not understand how or why there were so many presents under the tree.

My grandmother's combustion oven, that continually glowed embers for hot water, was fired up that Christmas as always to cook the fowl killed by my Pap, who set all his grandchildren up to pull out feathers. I hated the plucking of feathers, but I stood with the other children and pretended to help. We hung over the sinks, covered in floating feathers clinging to our arms and working in the warm water as we tugged the feathers out of the flesh.

That Christmas was the first time I saw my Pap kill hens and ducks for Christmas dinner. I was shocked and overwhelmed, and I ran away screaming as I watched a headless hen running around the backyard.

Another year, we visited my grandparents before Christmas, and this time they gave us a duck to take home to kill and eat ourselves. I remember the long ride home in the back on the truck tray, covered by a tarpaulin and cuddled up beside the duck that was to be eaten. It was not killed that Christmas as I protested too loudly with tears and screams. I don't know exactly what ever happened to that duck. I think it went to my aunt to live with her collection of fowls.

A memorable Christmas for me was also the last Christmas I spent with Ezara, my mother. I was pregnant with my third child as I took Ezara to do some shopping. She wanted to buy me a present. She had just been diagnosed with terminal cancer and she was very weak, but still she wanted to buy me a nice pot to put a plant in.

In the week before that Christmas, we arrived at the garden centre near her home. We found a medium-sized bright yellow pot that I loved. She bought it for me, and she told me, "Put a nice plant in it and can keep it in memory of me when I am not here anymore."

I loved it and carried it home that day when she could barely walk the short distance to her home.

She loved gardening, and I had been her helper since I was a small child. I remember my grandmother once created a beautiful pot of maidenhair fern in what she called her brass jardinière. She polished that container every week with a soft cloth until you could see your face in it. She watered the plant and kept her fern well-nourished and protected from any harsh weather. It responded beautifully to her loving touch.

Planting flowers and creating indoor plants was her love. I followed her lead and always had indoor plants and an outside garden until Nettie passed. My husband rescued all my plants when I gave up on them and then planted them out in the garden for me. He now does the gardening, as I have never returned to my rich pleasure of gardening.

On that Christmas morning, as on every Christmas morning, we drove the ten minutes to her flat to bring her home for Christmas—the last one before she would be taken to hospital for the final time.

But that is so long ago, and now I will delight in my own children, grandchildren, and great grandchildren arriving on Christmas day this year for our own Christmas festivities. I have ordered all my gifts online and my adult gentle son loved the time we spent together picking out the gifts. He waits with me each day as each parcel arrives. It is his greatest joy to collect the packages from the delivery van.

When they all arrive, we sit together and wrap his presents for the family, and he helps me wrap mine. To be part of his joy and believe in his innocent love of giving and receiving brings me to tears. It is not that he doesn't believe in Santa; he just believes that he is just too old for Santa. He makes everything into a celebration. Life itself is a celebration for him. With him, I have found my innocence in believing in becoming my soul every minute of every day. Without him, I would miss the joy of celebrating life as he does.

He looks forward to the cricket season, the football season, the latest DVD release suitable for him, the newest CD release for him, and family TV shows he likes. He makes every effort to make anything exciting during any day and turn it into an event worth waiting for. However, I miss half of the things that I could turn into events for myself and others. He is a joy in my life as he keeps me young and present in the moment. He lives from his soul and sees life through innocent eyes. He amazes me and the other members of the family.

To help him with his grief for his sister, he so willingly believed there is life in heaven when I told him she was in heaven. He has come to understand that bodies die and we live as our souls in heaven. This concept does not bother him. He understands that he has Divine help to get through his anxieties, fears, worries, and losses. He knows he is not alone with Jesus to help him. He tells me when Jesus has just helped him.

On one occasion when he was upset and couldn't get the upsetting thoughts out of his head (which is so difficult for a gentle soul to do), he came to me as I was watching a spiritual show and sat with me. I was silent and let the moment direct itself. Whatever was said on the show calmed him. He told me Jesus just helped him to calm down. He was amazed it relieved him. He repeatedly told me he was okay now because Jesus had helped him.

He is so in touch with the other side that I believe there is no other side, that it all exits here in the now. He keeps my faith alive each moment of every day. He seems so wise in his knowledge of the spiritual realm. Every Easter since he was little, I have always told him the story of Jesus and fleshed out more details for him as he understood more as he got older.

We start the story on Palm Sunday as Jesus is welcomed by everyone. On Holy Thursday night, I tell the story of Peter cutting off the soldier's ear, and Jesus healing the soldier by picking his ear up and placing it back on. He loves that bit, and retells it with passion and actions. Then he waits through Good Friday until we sit outside waiting for 3 p.m. to come, waiting for the time for Jesus to die on the cross. He knows when the wind stands still around us, that is when Jesus dies. My son feels Jesus walk past us with a cool breeze to acknowledge that he is still alive and with us.

On Easter Saturday, he rests and waits as Jesus is in his tomb all day resting. Then on Easter Sunday when Jesus has gone, he can have the Easter eggs that he can break open just like the angel breaks open Jesus's tomb.

I live a simple life with the gentle soul children. I am also a gentle soul in love with Jesus and Mary, and I have taught my children their love of the Divine through my love.

Chapter 16

NEW LIFE

My children and grandchildren are all amazed at my beautiful statues, paintings, and ornaments of the Blessed Mother and Jesus and his saints strewn throughout my house and out into my garden. There is no way of not noticing that the environment on our property has been established for the acknowledgment of the Divine Presence and his Mother's protection of our family and our lives together. It is a place of love to all family and others who visit us here.

At my age, I am still building a family of love, and a home of love that will outlive me. We have planted many trees that will offer shade to the young who will flourish when I am gone. We have planted fruit trees for sustenance for the young. This year, we will plant a Christmas tree that will be their hope for the future—a tree that will connect them to the past, present, and future. It will open many Christmas secrets for the young to learn and ponder. We must not leave an environment devoid of nourishment for the young.

My intention is also to plant hope for my children, in honour of my gentling soul ancestors and their efforts to build hope in a new life in a new country for us. I am truly grateful for their lives and for re-establishing a life possible for us to continue. If we continue to keep building hope for the new generations as they did, we will achieve peace across the nations.

We must tell our children how important it is to love and what it means to be void of love. Wars rage because of lack of love. Hatred begins with a lack of love for one another. Twisted hearts without love attack sensitive hearts. Anger embellishes entitlement, greed, intolerance, and jealousy and mocks open love.

All these vices can attack gentling souls, as they are not exempt from feelings of anger, jealousy, and other emotions. However, they find it difficult to act out these feelings because of the perpetual emotional heaviness constantly regurgitating in their minds and bodies. They cannot bear the pain of the heaviness, and they prefer to accept the embrace of love.

Each day is a calling to offer peace and love into the world, as Saint Anthony did. It is up to every one of us to offer love and accept an embrace of love instead of feeding the vices within ourselves. The simplicity of living in the moment with wonder and joy in my heart keeps me ever anticipating the miracle of what may happen next. There is no way of knowing what spirit will open each day in us by drawing the past together with the present and the future. There is only the unknown miracle about to happen.

Not so long ago, as I was shaving my adult gentle son's facial stubble, as I always do, I was thinking of his namesake, and then I was thinking of the painting of Saint Anthony over my bed. Then another thought struck me so quickly that it seemed to come from nowhere. I looked up deeply into my son's blue eyes (I am so much shorter than he is) and I suddenly thought to myself, *Who are you? Are you Saint Anthony?*

He instantly looked back at me, directly into my eyes, which is very unusual for a person with gaze avoidance like him. He looked at me with a knowledge of what I had just thought, and yet we said nothing to each other. I shuddered. *He is making eye contact with me for such a split second, but there it is,* I thought. I was left reeling with the dazzling awareness that I was right. *You are Saint Anthony acknowledging yourself to me,* I said to myself as I nearly dropped the razor. I quickly grabbed it again and finished off without cutting him.

My mind travelled to Saint Anthony. I realised that *as he was an advanced soul when he lived on earth centuries ago, he would most likely reincarnate as a gentling soul with an impairment that would stop him from having the earthly life he once knew. He just came to bring peace to the world by wanting nothing for himself from this world, only love and peace for others.*

My mind boggles. I say to myself, *How many other advanced souls have reincarnated as gentling souls throughout the world? This is not an impossible concept to believe.* I am astonished and faced with the reality of the unknown becoming known.

I finished my task and watched as he wandered off saying to me, "That feels better, Mum." I am left with an unbelievable impression of meeting and knowing an advanced soul intimately. After this day, my love for him ignited from a mother's love to the love of an advanced soul. I can no longer see his impairment. I can only see his mission here on earth as an individual soul who made the choice to come to earth with an impairment.

His coming to earth was impossible. Believing he would come, however, we had already prepared for him before we knew he was on his way. He is the man with a disability who I saw with Mary when she visited us many years ago in my front garden. Just recently, my husband reestablished her garden as I asked so all can see her as they arrive.

The souls of the conclave visit me now in my waking state, and I am used to hearing directions, answers, and warnings. Usually, they join me as I begin my nightly prayers, clustering together in my room while I am wide awake. They look like soft glowing orbs all moving together in the darkness of my sanctuary. There are so many of them. They are silent and communicate with me one at a time. I awaken each day after meeting with the elders in the heavenly realm. Our encounters continue during the day as I reinstate myself back into earthly living.

Presently, I know I irritate my family members as I am unresponsive to their small woes that I am unable to change. I am constantly finding my way through the passage of daily spiritual awakenings, which bring their own changes to me. I wait patiently for daily requests from Spirit and from my elders in heaven. They wait patiently with me for my next response to an important request from my family, colleagues, or others.

I do my best at work each day, as I am continually summoned to the work of my soul. I must answer for I have no peace of mind or soul if I ignore the messages coming to me constantly. Being constantly watchful for another message, as all messages are requests of angels, light beings, and Spirit, leaves me present and ready in the moment. I live from moment to moment with the hope that the future will uncover the means to bring love and peace to all I meet.

At times, it feels like I have been pushed off a racing train through the side door when I wasn't looking and landed in a strange environment. Many years ago, I had a dream of that happening and I did not understand what it meant. Now I am beginning to understand. I feel I have left the security of being on the train going to a destination of my own choosing. Now I have landed in a land where I have no understanding of my destination, other than to follow where I am being led. I am operating constantly in my soul, and I feel I must respond to the deep inner urgings of my gentling soul to be able to understand what is being asked of me.

Recently I came across the funeral notice of the husband of my long-lost sister Ralia. Ralia was given to my mother Ezara by her parents to care for when she was an infant. Ralia lived with us for eleven years, until one day she was taken from us and went back to live with her biological parents.

There was little contact with her until she married and had children of her own. Then, only her husband and children knew of her childhood with us. No one in her newly extended family and friends knew of her absence from her family of origin as a child.

I was overwhelmed and felt my soul immediately respond to the funeral notice. It gave details of how to find her. Nervously, I wrote to her of my enduring love for her, ensuring her that she is always remembered. Weeks later, I was contacted by one of her children telling me that their mother had passed only days earlier and that her funeral was to be in a few days' time.

I spoke for nearly an hour with her daughter and thanked her for answering my letter. I felt I had such a deep soul connection to her children and felt warmly welcomed into their family at this sad time. My heart was breaking for them as they had just lost both of their parents. She told me, "Mum would want you to come to the funeral. You are most welcome to come, but no one here knows of her past with you."

Once again, I felt cut off from Ralia. I was holding back tears when I replied, "I won't come, as I will probably cry, and no one will know who I am and why I am so upset." She then offered me the live stream link to the funeral so I could watch it in private. It is just as well that I didn't go because I burst into tears as soon as the ceremony started. I cried throughout the whole event. To see her again through her photos was our last connection. I know she was present in soul as we connected once more. Our souls will never be separated.

Another soul-filled incident happened just two nights ago. I was awake until midnight and as I turned to settle for the night, I was already praying. I was so heart-weary from the week's chaotic events at work, my sister's illness in her back stopping her from walking, and the inability to keep myself and everyone calm. I was processing slowly, as a gentle soul does. As I was still bothered, I asked in my prayers for these worries to be taken from me as I was weary of heart and had nothing left to give.

I tried to doze off to sleep but I couldn't get into a deep sleep. At 2.30 a.m., I was startled when my dog barked viciously from her basket at the end of my bed. She lies near the open door with the screen closed and obviously was warning me of something happening. I jumped up and turned on my bedroom light. My husband grabbed his torch and went to check outside. I ran to turn all the veranda lights on in case there was someone out there.

We unwittingly concluded that a car may have pulled up, as they do sometimes near our place along a country road, to check for directions and drove away. We went back to bed still believing something else weird just happened.

Of course, it was hard to get back to sleep after a startle, and it became a good time for me to check social media. I saw that I had received a message from my sister about midnight when I was struggling to sleep and praying for assistance for her.

She sent me a video clip from Lourdes where someone was investigating the miracles associated with Saint Bernadette and Mother Mary. I had given my sister rosary beads with Lourdes water in them for Christmas two days earlier. She was so emotionally taken aback with the gift. She told me that she truly loved them and would treasure them.

I answered her message by acknowledging the Lourdes story, and the fact that she pointed out to me that the case in the video became the seventieth miracle accepted at the waters of Lourdes. I told her that it is just like her diagnosis with her back and her inability to walk. I told her of my experience with my dog. I sent the answer to her message at 3.30 a.m., not expecting her to hear the message arrive, let alone answer me at that time in the morning.

Next thing I knew, she answered me. She told me that she too had been awake all night, trying to comprehend the message in the Lourdes story. Immediately, I knew it was a "Mary moment." This is what I call the presence of Mary when she comes in really close to tell me something special. I understood why my dog was barking, and as we were speaking, why my sister's cat was growling at nothing there.

Mary had heard our mutual prayers that we could not cope any longer and we needed a healing for our gentle souls. I believe with all my heart and soul that my sister and I had been heard and were each being offered a healing. We believe that my sister is on her way to being healed of her illness and I am being healed with relief. We promised each other to pray the rosary as we both fell asleep.

I was finally nearing rest as the sun began to shine through my window. I pulled the curtains shut and came back into bed. I finally fell asleep until 7 a.m., when the dog needed to go outside. I was having the family of twenty-two for secret Santa Christmas presents and lunch that day and I had to go back to sleep before they all arrived so I could stay awake for them during the day.

I awoke refreshed but lacking energy, so I let the others run the day with help from me, not the other way around. I was enthralled with the nightly meeting with my beautiful Mother Mary. I still needed time to understand her message to both of us. However, I knew it was an acceptance of our aging gentle souls and an understanding of our growing faith in her.

After Mother Mary's visit the other night, I see my sister use her legs to try to walk once more. I know what I need to do each day as the messages arrive. With each message I receive, I am guided to each task that I am to undertake, be it bookwork, washing, cooking, cleaning, praying, healing, and taking care of family.

I enjoy each day as heaven intends. I am thankful for all that has been given to me, all that I have waited for that is now being given, and all that I am still to receive. I enjoy the wait as I must finish off what I have started with the intention of letting heaven have its own life.

Today while lunching in the park, we witnessed heaven having its own life once more. We were amazed as four fully loaded passenger vans arrived to join us. Many gentling souls with their companions descended upon the ground in front of us as if they were arriving from heaven.

My gentling soul son eagerly watched each of them arrive and begin to meander around the park. No one spoke. As they settled, we became absorbed in each other's presence. Our energies became palpable.

My son spoke, "This is the place where I arrived from heaven to complete God's mission, and I will return from here when I am finished."

My surprise at his words ignited thoughts of the ancient conclave of souls. Were these some of the gentling souls from the conclave coming to celebrate with us?

We welcomed these souls into the huge picnic rotunda set among the shady mountain trees and dined together.

Chapter 17

EPILOGUE

Throughout this story, through the quiet, gentling souls comes the acceptance of the Divine's love for meek and humble souls. The Divine embraces the gentling souls who are left unscarred by the search for lives that will take them far from their souls. By giving up their lives of human "normality," they bring their sensitivities to imbue their surroundings with peace, tranquillity, and love.

As they have not availed themselves of the many unattainable desires and need for control presented in life for others, they are left only with their souls within impaired bodies. They come only to filter goodness and blessings onto the earth.

The gentling souls' presence here on earth with their protectors is to enlighten others. With the last gentling souls in this family, preparation has begun for future generations of companion souls to honour the gentling souls.

There is so much work to be done to reset the earth for the spreading of peace and love. It is up to the new gentling souls' companions to continue to permeate the earth with the gentle ones' love and peace. They will also teach what they have gained from being in contact with the gentle ones by carrying the gentling souls' banner high: "Only Love Unites Us."

There is nothing else in the gentling ones' lives, for all they seek from each one of us is "love"—to love them, to love each other, to love everyone. The gentling souls come to earth to be love with the only intention of spreading love. They seek to be loved in imperfect bodies by their parents, family, friends, and by every stranger they meet in their environments.

Love is all that is missing in a world of hatred, revenge, and war.

How do we spread the love? We become the love.

Imagine a life without impairments—no impairments in our bodies, our animals, our plants. This ideal of no impairments is innovative in a world where the whole purpose of science and research and technology is to live without impairments. Yet every day there is another impairment discovered with no cure available.

In a world of fear, hatred, revenge, and murder, impairments and differences are not acceptable. They are seen as unnecessary burdens, as mistakes in society. People ask questions such as, "Why are they 'the gentle souls' on earth? Where do they fit in to our society?"

However, in a world of love, their impairments are acceptable and honoured with the belief that there is no perfection in our bodies. We create perfection only with love in our souls.

A new world would be where all people accept the imperfections in humanity and love the imperfections instead of killing them out. We would love our differences in other nations, religions, genders, races, and our neighbours and families instead of killing them out.

The words of Spirit remind us that we are perfect already.

"Replace fear with love. It is the time for you all to reflect on yourselves as more than human beings. You are eternal beings. Your consciousnesses exist eternally. Your souls are the love of God. Love with your whole soul, your whole heart, and your whole mind. Love each other. The gentle ones are advanced souls who have chosen to be with you only to show you love."

This story tells us how and why the gentling souls and their protectors come to filter goodness and blessings onto the earth throughout repressed generations. The conclave of souls forged an impenetrable bond between generations when it brought souls together to understand what they were choosing to live throughout the earthly centuries. The full understanding of the miracle is that they are souls with their own choices to accept to live these important lives as gentling souls.

Our perspective of people with neurogenetic disabilities can change with the understanding of who they are and why they may have a disability. Our attitude can change the world from discrimination to love, from misunderstanding to acceptance, from hatred to love, from war to peace.

If we can see through the eyes of those who have no interest in taking from the world but only giving love to the world, our fears of not being loved will no longer exist. We will have all we need. Our impairments are our souls.

It doesn't matter what we call the source: God, Mother, Father, Brother, Sister, and all the names each culture and religion uses. The source is one. We are all one, children from the one source of love. The gentle souls tell us to bring together all peoples through our love of each other, through the love of all religions, cultures, and through love of all.

What difference does it make to know where and why the genetic impairment started in the family?

The answer is resolved in the outcome of the story. Knowing where a genetic disability has come from and why makes all the difference to those who are still living and to those who have since passed. It can heal both the living and those in spirit.

For those who are still living, it is the gift of understanding and the gift of forgiveness. We understand our ancestors had no choice but to survive the conditions of their lives without knowing what happened in their generations while they lived on earth. Knowing frees and heals the present generations by understanding the ancestors' decisions.

For those who have passed, our gift to them is our understanding and acceptance of their lives and our forgiveness for the choices that alleviated their pain of passing the impairment to future generations.

I was to learn the reality of becoming a gentling soul, a wife, a mother, a grandmother, and a counsellor, so I could tell others. I was to experience abandonment from family, isolation, separateness, and indifference. I was to experience poverty with those who were poor, abandonment with those who were abandoned, isolation with those who were isolated, and a disability with those who live with a disability.

Now in my later years, I revisit the first call to my gentle soul, and I still hear the same message today. Tell everyone about love that can be found through the blessings of loving Mother Mary. Go to her to find her son. He loves her as only a son can love His mother. She loves Him as only a mother can love her son. Through their family you will find the Source, you will find the Divine—the Father/Mother of all children.

Although I often talk of finishing off what I started before I leave the earth, I intuitively remember that nothing is ever finished as life continues, for we are eternal. There is nothing that cannot be achieved with the sincere intention of doing everything out of love and through the spirit, no matter the cost.

I believe Spirit started all the confusion inside me, and keeps the fire in my belly stoked. Spirit keeps me safe and protected, and brings me back from the "abyss of forgetting who I am" each time I near the edge of oblivion.

Mary's constant message throughout the story is to continue believing that she loves and protects the gentle souls who become overwhelmed with life and its challenges. Her love blesses the existence of the gentling souls, the conclave of gentling souls, of the many advanced souls, and the purposes of their lives. Her love also blesses the purposes of the companion souls to protect and love the gentling souls while on earth.

By looking after our gentle soul children as well as our gentle soul adults, they become imperative miracles to bringing peace into the world. Through their impairment and their simple lives, their purpose is to bring others to their souls. It is ours to understand the purpose of the simplicity of their lives as the Divine's love for each one of us.

Our worries and concerns of what will happen next must dissolve. Life with a gentling soul is life lived fully in the moment in the company of the Divine and awareness of the reason for the impairment. This unfolding story of their lives is so unique that it needs to be continued exactly as Spirit intends.

As I go on in my life each day, I realise that I no longer walk through the brokenness of the earth. I walk on the path designed for me. It is a path so beautiful yet wrought with pain and love and leads straight to the Divine Source. It is a path that is adorned with every creature and plant of nature. It is a path of all the colours and wonders that are set before me. It is a path of mystery and intrigue. In these gifts I will generously indulge.

Instead of being so anxious and fearful of all earthly wants and woes, I encourage each of us to gather the means to reap the generous life set before us. Give to others all that passes through our hands, for it is not ours, but ours to use to fulfil our lives. We will live on forever.

Let us ask to be healed of our fears of losing all we have. We should instead seek abundance for what we will need to continue our missions before we leave this place and return to the heavenly source.

May life continue to flourish within the gentling souls. May honour and love be given to the gentling souls. May love and Divine direction take us into the future.

May the groundwork be set through these words so others will come to honour the Divine presence and Mother Mary.

May all be done as it is intended for the advanced souls who have made this place their earthly home.

Direct us as we become our souls and continue to unravel the messages that will enlighten many souls to love.

In Your holy name we ask all this of You dear Lord.